C000214930

FILTH

Jonathan Meades is the author of *Peter Knows What Dick Likes*, *Pompey* and *The Fowler Family Business*. He has written and performed in some twenty-five TV films on such subjects as the utopian avoidance of right angles, vertigo's lure, beer and Birmingham's appeal. He is a columnist on *The Times*.

For more information on Jonathan Meades
visit www.4thestate.com/jonathanmeades

FILTHY ENGLISH

Jonathan Meades

FOURTH ESTATE • *London* and *New York*

First published by Jonathon Cape Ltd, 1984
This edition first published in Great Britain in 2003 by
Fourth Estate
A Division of HarperCollins*Publishers*
77–85 Fulham Palace Road
London W6 8JB
www.4thestate.com

Some of these stories have previously appeared in *Harpers & Queen*:
'Rhododendron Gulch', January 1982; 'The Sylvan Life', November 1982;
'Fur and Skin', December 1982.

The right of Jonathan Meades to be identified as the author of
this work has been asserted by him in accordance with the
Copyright, Designs and Patents Act 1988

A catalogue record for this book is available from the British Library

978-0-00-715643-6

FOR HOLLY AND ROSE

CONTENTS

Fur and Skin

Aniseed is inseparably linked in my mind to the bodies of
fallen women. It is the madeleine that evokes a Magdalene. I
know what you're thinking: dirty dog, flashy talk. I can get
flashier still. I can do it in French. If you do it in French it's
poetry. 'C'est la madeleine qui évoque une Madeleine.' Good,
eh? What about this then: *'Mon royaume pour un ours.'*
Good eh? Pat me then. Mind you, frankly I wouldn't: I
mean, give away anything, let alone a kingdom (I should be
so lucky), for a horse *or* a bear. Especially not a bear. Have
you ever got a whiff of a bear's breath? I have. That's the sort
of thing you get to smell in my line of business. Guess what
I'm in then. Go on. What d'you think my line is then,
squire? (I'm aping Stobey, the ape. Prod ribs.) Guess,
strewth, guess! (Prod kidneys.) Don't be a wal. A long one to a
primate you won't get it ... But own up, you know me
already.

Anyway, my Magdalenes — that's what they were, you
could tell because they all had their jars of ointment. And,
no, it wasn't feet they anointed. But otherwise they were the
very picture of that whore in her pre-penitent state. Pernod,
Ricard, Berger, Chinchon, all the gaudy bottles of Asturias,

9

fennel, fenouillette, Sambuca, ouzo, raki, the umbelliferous
Levantine plant, 16 March 1915, the Pharisees' tithes, check
trousers, the Albigensian dwarf Lautrec – these provoke,
without my bidding, a seemingly infinite parade of mental
tableaux showing women of all races (the erotic imagination
is a catholic and egalitarian machine) in their transports, in
beds, in ones and twos and threes, in clothes that don't keep
them warm, in novel congas with exotic companions ... I
have seen them too often, these scenes of complicated
abandon. Very lively, of course, but they pall. I often find
myself in them. There, that's my keen tongue, pink as a
shepherd's delight – I'm talking about the German
shepherd, you understand. And my teeth – fine and white
and you have to admire the canines. And my eyes, by
Dunstan! are decorative, semi-spheres of liquid amber. And
look at my spry pointed ears and my taut body and piston-
potent haunches. Look most of all at my glorious pelt.
'You're a furrier's delight,' Eva told me once, running a
blood-red nail across my tummy. Joking? I'd like to think she
was, but you never can tell with these boudins from Belle-
ville; they'll do *anything* to get their *appartements* on
Wagram or Kléber. I'll tell you later about some of the things
that Eva did.

There was a time when I hadn't even heard of aniseed. In
those days all I knew was the beach that was white and curved
like a paring from a giant's big-toe-nail. Out in the bay the sea
that used to be rivers and before that rain turned into white
horses – no wonder you people believe in progress. Rusty
and I rushed into the waves. We rolled and squealed and
tumbled. We boxed on two legs like the hares we had heard
about but never seen. The moon made the sea stretch this far
or *this* far and sometimes it over-stretched itself so that the
sand dried quickly, as if a cloud had rushed from in front of
the sun. In the half-wet sets our bodies made we'd lick the salt
from each other and dream – one dream for two – of how we
would emulate Romulus and Remus, be suckled by a she-
human, lead a belligerent band of sheep-dogs and found a
city on the site where we had been nurtured.

10

Alas, only one half of the first part of this attractive prospectus came to be, *viz.* I got to be suckled by a she-human, several in fact, want to know how many John and that'll be another kirsch-fantaisie. Thanks. What else was there? There were Rusty's footprints, there was his scent — no brother ever smelled sweeter, there were the cliffs (gnawed sponge-cake, green topping), there were the wind-twisted tamarisks. I can't remember a day when there wasn't at least a breeze. Sometimes the vital wind still gets my face, strikes it just as it used to all that time ago and everything comes back to me, even Stobey and Old Nunc.

It was Stobey that sold me into this life. I was outside Chatsworth early one morning and was, oh, playful as a pup when Old Nunc bellowed from within:

"'Ere, Stobey, where you lurking then my son?'

Stobey was lurking on a tattered Lloydloom just a few feet from me. The chair's legs were sunk deep in the ground beneath his weight and all around us the grass rippled the way that fur does when subjected to a wind-effect machine. He was fashioning a Jack-Me-Lad from an empty Players' packet. This was a base form of origami — a tear here, a notch there, a notch thus ... What it added up to was a device with which Stobey impressed people of his ilk in public houses. He would pull the sliding part of the packet and to his cry of 'Jack-Me-Lad' up would spring a sort of tumescent robot. (You can imagine what people of Stobey's ilk were like.)

He took no notice of Old Nunc's cry, just carried on, his tongue leeching towards his ear in artisanal absorption. Away in the middle distance, on the slab of concrete beside a communal tap, Rusty lay on his back with his feet cycling in air; he looked happier than I had ever seen him. Every now and then his legs obscured a midget's handkerchief of sail in the bay. Old Nunc called Stobey's name again, stretching the vowels into howling parade-ground diphthongs. Stobey clenched his jaw in irritation, stared at me through half-closed eyes and carried on again, this time whistling softly through the mauve chipolatas that God had given him in lieu of lips.

11

I suppose you might say that I brought it on myself. I was oh so rash to pay no heed to that dextrous bully's minatory squint: I knew what it meant. I knew that man had a massive capacity for spite. There was silence within. Old Nunc must have thought that Stobey was off performing one of the chores with which he filled his day when he wasn't reading *Glass's Guide* in the caballeros between Blenheim and Wentworth Woodhouse. I gave him away. I shopped him with a raucous peal, rruff, ruf rarf, rruff, ruf rarf. Old Nunc was at the door before the shadow of my last euphonic note had died away.

'You gone mutt 'ave you Stobey?'

He stood there with a pocket calculator and a cigarette in one hand and his new day's beaker of St Raphael in the other, glaring. Stobey was glaring too, at me. (Does *glare* suggest murderous intent? It's meant to, he meant it to.)

'Mhungry, I wan' breakfas'.'

'I'll go down the Bag's then,' said Stobey.

'Nah. I fancy armstrongs. Big plate o' them. An' lamb's ones. Not yer pig's. You go down Oliver's now and you tell 'im it's for me and not to give yer pig's. An' rashers, nice fat rashers. You say it's for me an' to give yer nice fat rashers.'

'Oh Christ Nunc on me muvver's spleen sfreequarers a bleedin' hour down Oliver's an' back.'

'Well you'd 'ave better get goin' then 'adn't yer. On yer bike my son.'

But Stobey didn't have a bike. He had the van but he had lost his licence and, as Old Nunc kept reminding him, he didn't know where to find it. Old Nunc peeled him a couple of corrugated banknotes.

He set off, trudging resentfully across the field in the direction of Osborne and Compton Wynyates. I trotted along beside him, pitying him for his frayed trouser cuffs. He aimed a couple of kicks at me but I was as agile then as I am, famously, now; he missed. I sprinted across the grass to Rusty and for a few moments (that become more precious and more achingly vivid as the years go by) we somersaulted through the air with the sumptuous harmony and synchronous ease that only those sprung from the same egg can achieve. (The dainty little leaps of circus poodles — topiary on four legs — are to our soaring arcs what Miss Mamie van Doren was to Miss Marilyn Monroe. I draw my simile from the cinema because that's my world, the world I frequent.) Then Rusty wanted to play Hunt The Stash — he longed to accompany a policeman like Constable Constable on a raid on a pop star's house and be the one to find the cache of drugs in a tooled box from Tangiers or to collar the roadie, a Stobey look-alike, as he tried to flush the lavatory. I didn't want to play, so Rusty searched for mines instead and I ran after Stobey, thinking as usual that the way *I* would like to serve society was as a blind dog, proud in my cream harness, leading my master with gentle dignity through teeming streets, happy to be the apex of the trinity (whose other parts are black glasses and white stick) that signifies sightlessness. Stobey made to hit me but I didn't flinch so he threw a stick for me to chase. I brought it back and as we turned out on to the road beside Harlaxton (unlet because of the traffic noise) he threw it again. High this time and looping and I was already in pursuit when it was still way up in the air. The slipstream of something vast and noxious shunted me across the verge, put my hair *en brosse*; shaken, I looked back at Stobey, who was grinning with canicidal glee, almost. The stick was now a mat of splinters in the middle of the road save for a cylinder of lichen-grey bark that bobbed about the tarmac. A belching milk tanker was racing away down the hill.

Stobey waited to be served behind a harassed slattern. Her little boy squatted on his haunches whining wretchedly about his bellyache and eating copperish rabbit droppings from a paper bag. The scattered sawdust was patterned like iron filings subjected to a magnetic field or like the stubble on the back of a madman's head. Oliver held up a red and yellow wedge that bled down his arm. A short man and a big blonde joined the queue behind me, they both wore scent, they both wore jewellery. The slattern picked up her package.

'Two pounda lamb's kidneys an' halfa streaky,' said Stobey.

13

'Cmon Lance,' said the slattern to her son who spilled his bag of rabbit droppings. They rolled all over the floor. I don't know what came over me; I didn't then, I mean. I do now. The smell of the things! Bliss! Olfactory wipe-out! Their perfume was not luxury, it was *necessity*. This was nosejoy as few know it. It was, of course, aniseed. I rooted, I slipped on the sawdust. Then I tasted and swooned, I hardly felt Stobey's boot as it connected with my shoulder.

The big blonde was tittering. The short man said:

'Impwessive ahnd you got there. Vewy intwestin' indeed. 'E's not for sale I don't suppose?'

Stobey and the short man huddled together under a picture showing a pig before and after its fatal accident. The big blonde gave blubbing Lance a coin. The short man spat on his fingers and, impeded only by his cluster of rings, counted a sum off a roll of notes so thick that Stobey gaped open-mouthed. I looked up and found that the big blonde was running her eyes over me in a most unusual way.

We do not gnaw bones because we want to, you know. We gnaw bones because they are all that we are given. We do not determine the course of our lives. The notion of *la carte* is foreign to us. We get what's thrown to us. Choice? Ha! We live in an open prison of the will. It's not for nothing that it's called a *dog's life*. It's not for nothing that *dog* is a universal word of deprecation. It's not for nothing that *dog* is synonymous with, variously, coward, churl, traitor, braggart, bully, head-case, shirker, spoil-sport.

Sammi and Lou promoted my fondness for aniseed. They gave it me all the time, in all sorts of ways; sometimes, I suspect, they tried to disguise the fact that they were giving it to me — this would be characteristic. I had Pal enriched with marrowbone jelly and ground aniseed balls. I had quivering bricks of meat and jelly smothered in pastis. I had mounds of Chum in which Sammi's surgeon-gloved hands had buried quantities of star anise that scraped my palate. I had everything Lou left on the side of his plate — and he liked to leave a

14

lot as a sign of his profligacy – covered in fennel seeds. Sometimes the water in my bowl was oily and viscous, which meant that a bottle of Sambuca had been tipped into it during the night by Lou as he stumbled about in his shorty towelling gown. After a few weeks during which my dreams grew increasingly lush and my waking life got ever more sybaritic – chocolate truffles, laps, pats, carpets with canapés to be found deep in the pile – Sammi and Lou returned with me to Back Up The Smoke. We sped past Harlaxton with my head out of the window over Sammi's shoulder and my ears swept back to render me the perfect paradigm of sleek streamlining. Rusty was nowhere to be seen but I hardly cared – I was intoxicated by my new life, I was in love with the future and all it held. Rusty was just part of the past, like the dank space beneath Chatsworth where we used to shelter from the stinging rain or like the mother that I had quite forgotten.

At Back Up The Smoke everything is red, dangerous, quick, loud, and the quoins, obeying a law of progressive diminution, march away to a horizon that is so close and dismal it is an obviation of all hope. There they fostered my addiction. They made me an *addict*. They made me dependent. Then they became dependent on me. They were, you see, parasites who had to create their own host – me, lucky me. I of course had no idea that I was dependent on aniseed till one evening when I realised that none of the dishes I had been served that day had contained a trace of the stuff and that I ached – sore head, intercostal neuralgia, tight hamstrings. That night I scraped the suede from the walls of Lou's pool room. The next day my food again lacked my drug. I further damaged Lou's pool room and again went unpunished. I could smell burnt flesh. Rats painted in gay Day-glo stripes sprinted along the pool table. A hairless man poked his head through the ceiling and said the Iron Duke was dead. I often shook. I lay on my flank and heard myself howl. I was locked in the room, my meagre rations were pushed round a just-opened door. One corner of the room I filled with brown coils. Then they came for me.

15

Two men, both of them unfamiliar to me, both of them wearing thick gauntlets in case I should sink my teeth into them, led me to the top of the house.

Although it was daytime the windows of this room were covered. The brightest lights I had ever seen were aimed at static white kites. Four men with bad eyesight stared at Sammi through complicated black spectacles. Although it was daytime she lay on a bed wearing a coat which looked as if it was made from the coats of my cousins. No doubt she is ill, cold, and these men are physicians: my thoughts ran thus, and their rightness was confirmed by the way that Lou consulted with each of these specialists. He looked worried. Then he smiled at me and leaned over Sammi. I couldn't see what he was doing, but I heard a seal break and I realised that he was showing the doctors where Sammi's pain was, just near her tummy. Then he said 'Shoot' and I ducked because I hadn't forgotten what Stobey was like with a gun and these men with their severe myopia were likely to be even worse. Then I smelled aniseed. Up on the downs are two identical tumuli, rosily autumnal. It must be that season because the copse that is way this side of them is crisp and russet. And the aniseed is just south of the copse.

But I must draw a curtain over this scene. From beyond the curtain you can, however, hear me panting, you can hear water lapping, you can hear Sammi humming, you can hear one of the doctors whistling 'My Ship Is Coming In', you can hear Lou saying 'That's my boy ... My Cwist this is goin' to be an earner ... Jus look at 'im go.' The film was, of course, *The Alsatian and Lorraine.* If you are shy about such things you can always attribute your knowledge of it to newspaper reports of the wrongful dismissal of twenty West Midlands car workers who spent their night shifts enjoying repeated viewings of it. Both Sammi and Lou were impressed by the counsel provided for the men by their trade union. He argued that given its high price, poor finish, lack-lustre design and the difficulty encountered in selling the model on which they were 'working' it was in everybody's interest that they should continue to watch films between their tea-breaks. The firm was censured and fined.

'That', pronounced Lou, jabbing the newspaper with his jet and sapphire finger, 'is just the sort of bwief we got to 'ave on *The Twue Meaning of Cancan.*'

Lou was having a spot of bother with a Watch Committee in the sticks on account of his – our? – follow-up to *The Alsatian and Lorraine*. This film made it clear that *cancan* is derived from *concon*. (The lexicographic wimps at the O.E.D. throw in the towel with a crummy 'said to be L.')

The pattern of my life was soon established: three weeks during which I was encouraged to indulge my habit; three unspeakable days of enforced abstinence; three or so days when I was allowed aniseed on the set but not off it. I was trapped. It was by these means that my best performances were coaxed from me. By the end of my first year I had appeared in many films, some of them 'genre classics', others ... Well, even such dogs as Lassie and Cerberus had their off-days. As my fame grew and more films and feats came between me and my pre-stellar self so did I increasingly yearn to be reunited with Rusty. And I'd have given it all up to be a blind dog, to have really *helped*. But I was, as I say, trapped by my addiction.

I suppose things might have been worse, they were to get worse. I was, however, immune to the diseases that are attendant on my kind of stardom. They are not transmittable to dogs. The spirochaete – the slow assassin that corkscrewed through Lord Randolph Churchill, Boswell, most poets, Frederick Delius, my precursor Errol Flynn and millions more besides – might know me but could never enter me. And just as I required no prophylaxis so could my co-stars dispense with the chemical and mechanical apparatus of contraception; my seed can do nothing to you people, don't worry. I should, I must admit, have liked to have been the co-author of one of those fabulous mixes – a head, say, like Delon's and a body like mine. Of course the hapless beast might have had the body of a Hitchcock or Welles and my head. The latter would, doubtless, have had the infinite sadness of G. F. Watts's *Minotaur*, but the former ... Oh,

17

what a big plump Whitstable his world would have been. And I should have liked my co-author to have been Eva; faithless, flighty, fickle Eva. You *dog. Volage!*

The ozonic bite of the breeze across a plain where a million ears of corn turned to listen as we passed by was the first sign I received that I was going home: I still thought of Chatsworth as my home. All they would have heard was Eva's invariable, promiscuous cry of '*Oh, comme c'est marrant — tu trouves pas, Henri?*'; she said this of every house, field, horse, church. I sat between her and Henri in the back of Lou's big, brand-new silver car which he had bought 'dead cheap, wock bom pwice', presumably because it had no roof — the workers, in all likelihood, had been watching *The Things Girls Do With Sauerkraut* when they were meant to be putting it on. Then the crust-gold fields gave way to the downs of my puppyhood, we reached the top of a hill and a wedge of blinding, mirror-bright sea appeared. My heart thumped. The sea came into and out of sight tantalisingly. I rode the green folds like a happy boy on a roller-coaster. Then we were surging along the road towards Harlaxton; I was all a-quiver; we rounded the bend, and it had gone. It wasn't there, and Audley End wasn't there, and Speke Hall and Wollaton ... they had disappeared. Where once there had been bright caravans and life and obeliscal chemical-toilet tents now there was nothing, nothing. A field, just a field. With cows in it. And where was Rusty? Where had my brother gone?

Eva's story was the story that I had heard from all my co-stars, with the exception of Glyn (*A Shepherd's Life*) who had never wanted to be a 'proper' actress and wasn't just filling in time before he got his break. Eva was unexceptional on that score. In every other way she was special. She was gentle, voluptuous, soft as milk; her self-interest was so patent it was touching, it informed everything she did. I thought she was lovely. I enjoyed making *Chien de Pompier* more than any other film. I enjoyed Eva more than any other co-star. She smelled so fresh and crisp and *biscuit-like* — this despite having only recently worked with a ram, a bear, a disgraced

18

zoo-keeper, twin midgets and lots of charcuterie. Henri, I am sure, was aware of my infatuation. His small eyes, whose parchment bags advertised some hepatic cock-up, followed us as we ran together along the beach, with me vainly searching for a sign of Rusty and her pretending, I suppose, that she was playing the climactic scene of a cinematic romance and that Trintignant or Depardieu was bounding through the edge of the spray towards her.

We made the film in a former aircraft hangar that sat baldly astride an old runway, where tansy and thistles grew. The runway ran to the sky in both directions; when the doors at both ends were open the effect was disorientating, disconcerting. I spent hours between takes lying in Eva's arms, snuggling greedily against her, gazing up at the far-off reflection of us together in the vast mirror that was suspended from the building's superstructure. This mirror was the biggest that anyone had ever seen; Lou was proud of that. It was, along with the fire-engine, the film's most important prop. I thought that we looked just right together. (I felt like a prince. The conjunction of fur and skin is a happy one.) Eva would blow into my ear and, rapturously, we would rehearse while the technicians – concave-chested men with Capstan hawks and meat-beaters' eyes – hooted and hissed and whistled and stamped. Henri would strut about threatening the sack to anyone who so much as took a swig of the many Marie Brizard anisette bottles that rested in a corner. Supine and sated, I stared at my twin on the ceiling; it was as if Rusty had found his own paramour and was forever fixed in vertiginous sprawl with her. I was happy for him.

Eva told me all about Henri, then we rehearsed again. (*Répétition*, apt word.) Henri, she said, was a jealous man. He was also a greedy man, and a cynical one. His cynicism had made him his first fortune. Did you ever meet a Frenchman who wasn't a hero of the Résistance? Who hadn't strangled a battalion of Boches with his own hands? Who didn't have an inventory of marshalling yards, bridges, barracks and canal basins that he had blown up? Who didn't have a tattered photograph that he'd pull out at every opportunity to show him wearing a beret and a bullet belt, clutching a sub-machine-gun, standing with his Pétaino-phobic dog in a landscape of maquis and rocks? Henri took that photograph. He took thousands. He transformed men who had sold their daughters to Hansi and Karl Heinz for half a pound of butter, men who had betrayed their brothers, men who had led the soft life, into men who might walk proudly through post-war France.

I'd have drawn the line at participating in those photographs. Henri's baseness made me love Eva all the more, and when the last scene was shot and the coughing onanists began to dismantle the set that had been our home I wept. The bed, *our* bed, that blissful site was perfunctorily wheeled and carried to a van that waited down the runway — the surface was too pitted to drive it any closer. The fire-engine was parked in long grass beside the runway. The sound-recordist carried away his worn machine towards it. The vast mirror was lowered from the ceiling, five crouching men moved it slowly past me; I was thankful that its black back was towards me and that I was spared the sight of my abjectness.

Eva and Henri were embracing, his hands moved beneath her clothes making the material jut and bulge like inarticu-late puppets; she giggled and sighed. My tongue was still numb with anisette, I could still taste her, my coat was smooth where she had pulled some goose-grass from it, the body that I was forced to occupy was the one that only minutes before she had toyed with languorously, dextrously, savagely. Lou sloped away with his arm round Sammi, telling her that he had heard about a book called *Ken-nelworth* that might make a good film. I was desolate. I walked hang-dog away past the fire-engine through canyons of tickling grass.

Then I heard it. A bark that rose and rose sweetly as if carried by cherubim. It was a bark that was an echo of mine. I turned, and there, back beyond the red and chrome appliance near where the van had been parked, was my double, my twin, my brother Rusty. As one we set off towards each other, matching each other sinew for sinew, muscle for muscle; our rhythm was as balanced and harmonious as it had been the last time we tumbled together — how long ago was that? And how long it seemed, that spring towards eternal reunion. He got bigger all the time. Now I could see his bouncing pelt and his springy tongue. Now I leapt, straight from stride into air. And he leapt as I leapt. He had been crying too — I could see his eyes. They were the last thing I saw. I went, they tell me, straight through the mirror (which disobligingly turned out to be made of tingling splinters) and discovered that on the other side of the looking-glass there is, aptly, blackness. Also there was the van and the sound-recordist with his tape of my voice; he got cut.

Some of the shards that pierced my corneas were as fine as hair and are still there. Giulia gives me pills for those times when it gets bad. I wish I could see her. I'd like to see her leading me, the blind dog, to Lou's new studio where we are making *Hot Dog, Sausage Dog*. Is she as bad and lovely as Eva? Please tell me. Her scent is that of aniseed.

The Sylvan Life

A chicken that is killed by being swung round and round by the neck will evacuate itself and so leave a thin cloacal trail all across the walls and the ceiling (the colour of a diseased lung) and across the bursting sofa and the happy family gewgaws and the nicotine brown photo of the Saints and the pin-up photo of the girl in the peanut adverts (dead now – tuinol and gin) and the poker-work antimacassar stapled to the door and across the matted slab of carpet and the ragged hairy moist rug pile where the cats slept and the meat-encrusted plates they ate off and the mallets and the axes and right across the mirror whose lost silvering already gave it the look of a slide constellated with gonococci. Also: when a chicken is killed by being swung round and round by the neck there will be a noise from Hell and air that is thick with dirty down. A chicken's neck will, in extremis, extend to a length of twelve inches; it will go that far to cling on to life, a chicken. Wendy knew that. There was nothing she didn't know about killing chickens. She knew the lot – she knew the lore, the practice, the tricks, the griff. Heaven to you and me might be a place where sloe-eyed exquisites happily respond to the old cry of '*à genoux, c'est l'heure du pipe*' but to Wendy it's

22

somewhere with a plenitude of fowl to strangle. I hope she's happy there.

She learned to kill a chicken when she was seven. When she was twenty-three she scored an own goal; it was her first and final go at denying her life. In between a lot happened to her. When she was thirteen her art teacher Ivor (ursine and bibulous and fond of knitted ties – this is supposition, I've never set eyes on the man) told her that she looked like Simonetta Vespucci. 'Bottiwho?' asked her father and gaped at the postcard she had given him. He stared and stared and turned it over and stared at the title, name, date as if he could understand them. He moved his lips in dissimulation of his illiteracy, which was unadmitted between them; if he wanted something read to him (about the Saints or the sales at Beaulieu Road, that sort of thing) he would say that his eyes hurt. Wendy didn't mind, this was the way fathers were, this was normal. She was a bit like that.

The winter she was six the child who sat next to her in class walked to the teacher's desk and said gravely: 'Wendy's got a tail, Miss.' Beneath the hem of the papery cotton frock she wore the year round there hung a hank of greyish fur. Her father, blindly doting and prescient of Jack Frost, had sewn her into the untreated skins of rabbits that he had trapped. She looked pretty as ever, if bulky. Her skin grew sore and it itched; she found gaps between the furs to stick her fingers through and she scratched and scratched. The many fleas and things that had been parasitical upon the rabbits took revenge on behalf of their dead hosts. Her skin got ulcerated. She fidgeted so. She didn't complain because it is cold in the Forest in winter and, anyway, how was she to know that this wasn't what you wore when you were six.

She was sent to live with the woman who was her mother. She didn't like it. She didn't like the vast giddy pile of stiff hair on top of the woman's head and she didn't like the things that must live in its caves and re-entrants. She didn't like the dull gust of smells when the woman put her face close to hers; she smelled like that, Wendy knew, because of the small bottle she held to her carotid pulse and because of the big bottle she

held to her mouth — sometimes she held one or other bottle
up to the window light, tipped it, peered at it, hurled it at the
wall. Wendy didn't like that. No, and she didn't like the
noise and the other children in the house. They tumbled
screeching down the stairs, clutching sticks and bits of broken
brick, their mouths stained by stolen sweets. When Wendy
asked them if they liked her they cackled echoically: 'Do you
like me ... Do you like me ... ' Another thing that she didn't
like was all the uncles who came to see her mother;
sometimes as many as six uncles would come between
teatime and bedtime. She marvelled at the size of her family
and wondered why none of her uncles had come to visit her
when she had lived in the Forest and why none of them had
news of Da, Keith, Wm and Bon.

At her new school she boasted about the number of uncles
she had. The other children were impressed when she told
them but the next day a little boy punched her on the side of
the head and said: 'Your mum's *approzzy*.' Wendy didn't
know what *approzzy* meant but she knew it must be bad
because her classmates whispered it and laughed and
prodded her. She wondered if it had something to do with the
woman's hair-do and asked one of her uncles, who replied by
telling her about the bakery where he worked. Soon after, the
teacher told them about Holland — dyke, finger, clog,
tulip — and then told them to draw a picture of a flower
seller. Wendy got it wrong and drew a picture of sacks of flour
being nibbled by rats. Everyone laughed at her again; the
sisters who crackled when they walked because of the
newspaper beneath their clothes pinched her during break.

Her truancy became chronic. She spent many days at
Bevois Valley climbing through the dead people's furniture
that was strewn across the pavements. A woman with saveloy
fingers pulled her out from beneath a gateleg table, said she
was a street arab. The sky was thick with tramlines and
rattling black cars hurtled down the hill; Wendy ran. She
trod on so many cracks that the bears or Boney or the Bogey
were bound to get her. She found herself surrounded by the
biggest buildings she had ever seen, abominable places that

emitted yellow steam and fearful shrieks; there were no windows, so the inhabitants must all be blind. She shivered and fled. Cowering on a wharf she watched the floating bridge coming towards her across the choppy water (pewter grey, white carets). Just wonder at how she must have felt when she saw that the vehicle at its prow was her father's truck with its load of scrape and a trail of gulls. That was when her father took her back to the Forest and taught her to kill chickens.

Forest no more signifies a tract of dense and unrelieved woodland than, say, Jambon de York means that the pig, the fibres of whose dead cured thigh are just now filling your molar cavity, lived its life at that northern city. Much of the Forest is heathland whose acid, inhospitable soil supports gorse, heather, bracken; it is of little agricultural or silvicultural use. There are, too, large areas of bog in whose depths there no doubt lie the twisted leathery bodies of ponies and of the men who tried to steal them by night. Now at night the sky is lighted by the flares of Fawley; those parts of crude oil that cannot be made into petrol or plastic or soap or polythene become the stuff of an elemental pyrotechny that may be witnessed from the Pepperbox near Salisbury, the Eyre Coote monument, Portsdown Hill, The Needles, all the south ...

By day the flames disappear into empyreal oblivion. It was by day and from near the source of these wonders that Wendy watched the glinting silver flying-boats swanning it in front of the vast hospital where lay all the soldiers whom Victoria and her successors considered too horribly maimed to show themselves in the world again. It made Wendy think about monarchs, and so did the brutal game of Rufus and Tyrrell that Wm and Bon used to play – this game was a variant of Cowboys and Indians and a precursor of Pickets and Scabs; and it made Wendy think about those poor soldiers. What would she have thought about this card, despatched the year she became a New Elizabethan? It is postmarked New

Milton and addressed to a destination near Reading: *You were quite right. It's lovely. Dennis has a bit of difficulty getting down the steps because they're so worn away. But once he's down on the beach he can take his leg off and just slide down into the water. I'd quite forgotten how lovely the Forest is and Dennis is most taken not having being (sic) here before. He says we have to watch what we eat because you never know if they're serving up pony. I can't remember if I ever told you but the last meal he had in France before he stepped on the mine was horse. But he's always embarrassed about that so mum's the word. Love to you both and the boys. Rene.*

On the obverse are told the institutionalised iconic lies that are invariably told of the Forest; four photos are arranged round an ovaloid device announcing that 'It's Fun To Be Here'. They show: a beach with groynes; a cerulean pond; a cute pony; a cute cottage. The pony's heavy fringe and the cottage's deep thatch lend the artless thing a sort of rudimentary symmetry. There is a lie on the other side too; Dennis lost his leg when he was AWOL and drunk and being chased by a military policeman — he ran in front of a blacked-out Catering Corps truck. You'd have thought that was punishment enough (prosthesis, fear of being rumbled) without what happened to him in the Forest.

The next year Irene wrote: *We've really fallen in love with the place all over again that Dennis is talking about moving down here. He says there are real prospects if you adopt a modern outlook. He'd love to be his own boss again like he was when he was in barbed wire so we've been looking round at some of the stores that are for sale. It's quite an adventure I can tell you. One place we looked at was just down the road from the picture. Must go now. Dennis is playing that 'Shut the Door, They're Coming in the Window' on the portable. It gives me the creeps. Love. Rene.* The picture she refers to shows a gleambright Vauxhall Cresta negotiating an 'Irish' ford; beside the ford is a bridge of reinforced concrete with pebbles set into it. Against its tubular railing lean two boys with their backs to the camera.

Watch Wm and Bon come to life, walk off the bridge and

up the stream. This stream is called Hucklebrook or Huckles Brook; I used to cycle to it on my carmine and white Raleigh Spacerider and swim in it at Ogdens where at certain pools it is four feet deep and was home to darting brown trout, a species that seems to have disappeared from our tables to make room for its ill-flavoured, prismatically coloured, intensely cultivated cousin (more of whom later). Wm is the one with close-set eyes behind glasses that have lenses thick and distorting as boiled sweets; Bon has other handicaps, his brain for instance. Here they come now, stalking up the bank of Hucklebrook, kicking at dry pony dung just the way Duncan Edwards would, screeching at bushes to flush out the birds, bunging stones into the water, signalling each other to shush when they see an emmet or a grockle (I'm well away by now, gliding – look, no hands – past the stables that became a dude ranch). A man exhibiting the furtive confidence of the daylight robber is digging up turfs with a hoe and a spade; he has no turbary rights but he does have a Morris 1000 pick-up and a grassless garden. He nods a guilty greeting to Wm and Bon. Wm makes a hissing sound and Bon makes a noise that sounds like 'Sarp, sarp, dewarra'.

Now in the stream there is a creature splashing violently, throwing up roly-poly pompadours of water. Bon gapes at it, jigs gawkishly, says something that suggests aphasia or a forgotten, distant tongue and jumps into the stream. He's wearing a shirt and shorts and scuffed black daps so there's not much to worry about and, besides, the goal is worth it. It is an eel with an L-shaped bone jammed in its jaw. It is bucking like mad to try to get rid of the thing, there is nothing slithy about it, about the way it writhes – as though it was hauled to and fro by a demented puppet master. Poor thing; it has spent almost three years crossing the Atlantic; it has undergone at least one change of sex; it has ignored the lure of the Fal, the Dart, the Exe and Frome; it has safely avoided the traps at Purewell and Ellingham; it has achieved maturity among green weeds. And now it has this trouble with a pork chop and a mad boy jumping up and down on top of it; further, it soon has another boy, more methodical, hitting it

27

with a spade. Even after all chance of its return to the Sargasso has gone and Wm has decapitated it with the astonished digger's hoe it keeps wriggling, which is perhaps as well because it shows the publican to whom they sell it (2/7d after haggling) that it's fresh. This is one of their first essays in commerce and it excites them.

Elephantiac beeches whose bark is scarred like the decoratively mutilated faces of African women dwarf the houses that are set among them in the north of the Forest. These houses are of a rudimentary sort, made from a variety of materials — corrugated iron, planks, bricks, telegraph poles, asbestos sheets, breezeblocks, reconstituted stone; some of them were railway carriages a long time ago but they have none of the airy elegance of Edwardian summer-houses converted from such stock. You will see there a lean-to built against another lean-to, here a tarpaulin roof. Every place seems to be in a state of constant repair or haphazard expansion. Everywhere are piles of building materials and pyramids of soggy orange-sprouting sand. There are rusted lorries with moss on them; gardens full of scrap metal; fences on their sides; rotting outhouses; broken and bulging hedges with their gaps plugged by wheel-less barrows, mattresses, tyres, anything. There is no paint that is not crazed and flaking and matt with age. Walk around and you'll find burnt-out cars, bramblebound greenhouses, a former garage signalled by a pitted, horizontal petrol pump. Walk on up unmade roads and men with sump oil in their hair and very off-white string vests may appear from cabins. Listen — no, not to the howl of ill-fed and murderous Alsatians pacing and scraping in cages fashioned from Borstal gauge wire, but to a desperate cooing, like that of a dove who has lost her love. Avert your eyes from that pony — it is suffering from the sores called galls and has a suppurative ooze, maggot-white and thick, coming from a fissure on its right hind coronet. And do not look on the sows with which it shares its boggy paddock; these beasts are as big as it is and roll in their own excrement which hangs in mucoid filaments from their snouts and

28

distended teats. Rich ochreous fungal growths obscure the stencilling on a big cable drum that lies in the ditch to your left.

I should turn back now: you don't want to see another caravan full of nettles, another veteran Elsan, another crowded washing-line stretched between a cracked drainpipe and a barren plum tree. And you most especially do not want to see another man with half a pound of margarine on his hair (you really cannot tell the difference, Wendy couldn't), like the one just coming round the side of his yellow and lime and pink metal bungalow with a lump of camshaft in his hand – does he always strike the water butt that way? You really should turn round. You are not welcome here. And, besides, this road soon turns into a mere track through a coniferous enclosure where dead crows are hung by wire on fences as if they are getting a posthumous garotting. Go back and try to figure what that cooing noise is. Try to figure too why these settlements on the northern side of the Forest have names like Nomansland, Lover, Canada, Bohemia, Sandy Balls (where, aptly, there used to be a naturist reserve).

When Dennis and Irene moved there they tried to find out, at least Irene did; it was her way of saying 'hello' to her new home. She didn't know about things like the Victoria County Histories or those little, invaluable booklets produced by Women's Institutes. She relied on what was not then called the 'oral tradition', i.e. she asked her few customers toponymic questions and got answers ranging from the philosophical ('Well, take a look round, eh' – Wendy's father) to the incomprehensible ('Rup trut, rup trut' – Bon) to the sound ('That's wha' it says on the signpost at Landford' – Wm). Her predominant memory of Wm and Bon and Wendy as children is of their taciturnity, their *exclusivity* – they appeared to discourage the society of other children.

Irene's retrospective suspicion is that this was at their father's behest: 'Of course we never knew what was going on. You never think of things like that but when it came out I wasn't surprised to tell you the truth … You know, you think back and you think aah yes. We just thought that they were a bit simple if you follow me. Dennis used to call them the

29

rude sons of the soil. If there was children come in the shop when Dennis was telling one of his stories – some of his stories were a bit saucy you see – I used to say, Not in front of the renchild Den. That's children backwards. But with them I didn't bother. Straight in and out they'd be, wouldn't pay no attention to anyone in the shop.'

The shop is still there, a bald square redbrick building of two storeys; it is largely unaltered since Dennis died and Irene moved away, since in fact it went self-service in 1959 and Dennis had his picture in the *Grocer* alongside a store entitled 'War Hero Brings Contemporary Approach To Rural Retailing'. The photo shows Dennis standing in front of and slightly to the east of the shop indicating its brand new plastic fascia with a gesture that is marine semaphore for C and 3. That page from the *Grocer* is framed and yellowing on Irene's sitting-room wall. It commemorates both the beginning of a prosperous period for them and the arrival of the first envelope, which was delivered at the same post as the half-dozen copies of the *Grocer* that Dennis had ordered up from London. The envelope was strangely stained and was addressed in an awkward, ill-controlled child's hand. It smelled terrible. Dennis was comparing the print quality of the copies of his photograph when Irene opened it and found that it contained the liver and claws of a chicken. When – to get fancy about it – the happy skin of everyday banality is burst by the bounding spleen of the phenomenal you remember it well. The minutiae of the moment remain fixed, will play eternally in your inner cinema. Thus Irene is a constant witness to the way Dennis tweaked his nostril hairs like a R.A.F. man might his handlebars – she had never seen him do that before. And the livers, they had an almost nacreous sheen on them. Most of all she remembers this: she followed Dennis out to the dustbins at the back and there, up in the beech that stood on the boundary of the two properties, sat Bon. Dennis, despite everything, waved to him. Bon held up the metal framed bow he carried for games of Rufus and Tyrrell and mimed firing an arrow at Irene's head. She is certain of that; his eyes were looking along the line of the imaginary missile straight at hers. Then he dropped to the ground via the top of the stout fence that Dennis had erected along the line shown in the deeds. He scampered away and that is how Irene remembers the first envelope.

Scrape. There are two sorts of scrape in this account of the Forest — I except of course those that the people got themselves into. (Really, they didn't know better.) The first sort is the one made by the feet of deer at the places where they urinate; like the soil it is brown and it is here merely as local colour. All local colour in the Forest is impasto, most of it is brown — every shade from sienna through oxblood, axeblood (*he left a tell-tale stain on the blade*), amber, beer, dirt to bitter choc (*né* nigger). All four species of deer that are found in the Forest are brown — the red deer is tan going on chestnut. There are presently about 1,500 deer in the Forest, in the approximate proportion of one male to two females — with the exception of the roebuck, bucks and stags are polygamous and incestuous. Each year something like a third of the population is culled by agents of the Forestry Commission and tenders are invited for the meat, which is usually exported to countries with a greater appetite for it than the British have or to countries which are willing to pay higher prices than the British are. The latter is possibly more likely for, *according to a survey*, 40 per cent of British homes now have deep-freezes. Now, that vast cubic capacity must surely be used to accommodate something other than catering packs of fish fingers, cwts of krinklekuts, bollards of mince, animal fat and food dye in buckets labelled ice cream (more, later), breaded goujons of plaice, jeroboams of creme made from the blood plasma of horses, lamburgers and so on. It *is* used for something else, and I'm not talking about gelignite (Kilburn etc.), about the truncated limbs of hitchhikers (caravan sites etc.), about car-flattened pheasants (everywhere). I am talking about sides of beef, whole sheep, half stags, real meat.

Listen to this. Steven Walton who lives in what is,

according to the Poet Laureate and all our eyes, the second most splendid house in the north Wiltshire town of Highworth used to park his not much less splendid motor cycle against the railings outside it. Late one night he was drinking in the Berkeley Poker when a swaying, importunate man approached him: 'That's your bike, isn't it, down the road. Want to sell it?' No, he didn't want to sell it. 'I really want that bike.' Steven left the pub and the man followed him: 'I really want it. I'll give you cash. Now. I'll put it in the back of my van.' The man then did two things. He took a roll of £20 notes from his shirt pocket and offered to count out £1,500 ('not a bad price') on the bonnet of a car. The second thing he did in confirmation of his earnest was to point out to Steven his 'van'. It was an unmarked pantechnicon van, of the sort used by furniture removers. Steven looked at the man, who had the thickest glasses he had ever seen: 'Do you always drive about in a thing like that?' Incredulity on both sides. The man replied: 'Don't be soft. Me and my brother are just going up the Cotswolds to shoot some sheep.' This is when Bon limped along with a bag of fish and chips as big as a baby. He was pleased to show Steven the armoury they had in the cab of their vehicle: a ·22, a ·303, a crossbow. Steven did not sell his motor cycle, it was stolen a few weeks later, the chain attaching it to the railings snapped by what (a man from Thamesdown Police told Julia Walton) was 'a feat of superhuman strength'.

That was the only time that Steven met them; when I knew them they were poachers, not rustlers — there is a difference. Humping a sack of warm and bleeding stag Bon would appear at twilight at the houses of people he had hardly met. He was taking a chance, though even now the fine for poaching deer in the Forest rarely exceeds £20. His sales pitch was a face that promised actual bodily harm to anyone who dared send him away without having bought a chunk of meat. He drank away his gains in dipsodality at a rudimentary pub which sold a dense, opaque scrumpy. This stuff was fortified by lumps of rotting meat and the bodies of vermin. (It was by no means the strongest intoxicant that played in

Bon's brain.) Just as alcohol and atropine alter behaviour and sight so will an electric saw and an axe alter a just-dead beast, turn it into a saleable commodity that is *unrecognisable* as the sheep that was in your field an hour ago. Here is the beauty of this sort of crime, in the swiftness of the transformation: sheep shot in a field at Stow-on-the-Wold are halal mutton in Birmingham an hour later. It takes half an hour longer to change a Forest buck into London venison. This is rustling. This is business.

The motorways have been a boon and so have infra-red telescopic sights and crossbows. The I.R.A. has helped too (explosives, ammunition, etc.). Wm and Bon have also done trout farms, prize bulls, turkeys (seasonal), ducks, goats, guinea-fowl, salmon (with both dynamite and poison), pigs, ponies (for sport rather than profit). They have good contacts now and will obtain venison the year round. They only rarely eat what they take, they prefer to load their freezer with stuff from the cash and carry near Eastleigh; they no doubt have nothing but scorn for those tyros who kill and cut up animals in the field, leaving red and white entrails like shredded ensigns on the hedgerows. Watch the greedy crows gobble the lot. Watch the greedy crows in autumn as the velvet cover of antlers hangs like dreadlocks from new tines whose strength is determined by testosterone (within) and limestone (without). Watch them gobble it when it falls on the leafmeal that is broken here and there by the bulging, seductive, polka-dotted fruit bodies of Amanita muscaria. Look away genteel reader, because the big buck with a warbler on its bez-tine is just now emitting a steaming picric stream of what may be hallucinogenic waste. Here and there the forest floor is starred with scrape. And not far away, beyond the bounds of this enclosure, Wendy's father's truck is creaking beneath the weight of the stuff.

This is the second sort of scrape. It is caterers' slang, this word, for left-overs, peelings, rinds, skins, outer leaves, gristle, shells, stems, entrails, scales, heads, bones, pips, stones, tails, etc. — everything that goes into the kitchen save that which goes away in the punter's bulgy tum. (According to Vyle in *The Complete Gastrophone*, 4 vols, New Haven, 1971–5, scrape is so called because 'it is characteristically *scraped* from the plate (q.v.) or preparation area (q.v.) by a skiv (q.v.)'. The earliest illustration he cites is a figurative one, from Dick Holl's *The Grand Rapids Slayings*, 1938: '"Blow!" she snarled. "You crock of scrape."'') Bad life imitates bad art: at several of the cafés, restaurants, canteens, institutional and school kitchens, messes and milk bars from which he collected the scrape, Wendy's father was known as 'Scrapeface' or 'Old Scrapy' or 'The Scrapeman'. These were not affectionate sobriquets. They were the inventions of foul-mouthed crones with washday-red hands and nylon turbans, whose conversation was of gynaecological calamities and feeble husbands; they measured men against Troy Donahue and Ty Hardin and Tab Hunter.

Wendy's father was found wanting. He was dour, furtive, wiry, pale, with the air of a dog that has been kicked a lot. His flat cap was dark with haircream. His clothes were ragged and filthy. And his truck, oh, his truck. It moved slowly, slowly through the amber naves of the great Forest avenues with more flies than anyone has ever counted littering its bacterial rick, buzzing above it in phalangeal swarm. In the waste of a thousand tables that was stuck to its sides and doors and tail-board you could discern faces, animals, clipper ships – the leguminous jesting of Arcimboldo aped by random combination.

It must have been from Wendy's father that Wm and Bon got their commercial acumen. He was paid to take away the stuff and paid again by the piggeries to which he delivered it. Anyone who had pigs knew Wendy's father. He brought scrape to places where there wasn't any. No one else did. Six days a week he collected, six days a week he delivered. It is true that the stuff he delivered wasn't always what he had just collected. The rick was eternal, self-renewing, but at its bottom there was matter that had been there for years in a state of perpetual metamorphosis and unrecognisable now as yolk, lights, hoof, cabbage. This core was rarely dis-turbed – it depended on how much he got, how much he

sold. He was a king in this world. The seventh day he
sometimes took Wendy to the seaside or to see the flying-
boats or to Great Yews where the boles of the trees were more
swollen than those of any in the Forest and where there were
the ruins of a house called Vanity. He always took her
somewhere to post the envelope and she loved writing on it.
Once he had to brake so hard that she fell forward and hit her
head. He got some moss and made her hold it there and the
next day no egg had grown on her brow.

Although Wendy's father couldn't read he liked books. He
liked *Saucy, Spicy, Naughty, Nice, Ooh La La, Continental
Miss, Stocking Studies, Briefs Encounter*. He was an expert
on June Palmer. He adored her hairlessness; she had been
airbrushed into perpetual prepubescence. He often
wondered, I expect, why the girls in the books he liked – had
he been able to read he'd have known about their exciting
lives, all speed boats and split-level apartments – were hairless and why Wendy's mother hadn't been. This is probably
the only thing he had in common with John Ruskin, who
thought female statuary was that way out of naturalism not
pudeur and never recovered from the revelation of Effie's
dark wedge.
    Whether his incestuous kinship with Wendy was pro-
moted by the fact of her infantile sex's illusory cor-
respondence to those he protractedly gaped at is moot, for it
did go on after she had reached puberty. (It seems that she
accepted it all unquestioningly till she was fourteen. When
Keith had gone away to sea Wendy's father had told her to
move in with him so that she would no longer have to share a
bed with Wm and Bon.) Of course he was familiar with his
daughter's nakedness; when her mother had left he had
diligently changed Wendy's nappy every couple of days and
the *order* of her pubic symphysis enraptured him in a way that
was precursive of the graver, baser delight he would take in
her frail body. There are other things to consider.
    (a) It may just have been lust or a mix of desperation and

35

lust. The unavailability of potential legitimate sexual partners is a common enough provocation to incest and such partners were unavailable to Wendy's father, not least because he smelled of his truck.

(b) There is a *tradition* of incest in the Forest; and traditions are, characteristically, transmitted by parents to children. So the proscription of incest is weak; it is an act that has attained an ordinariness because of the frequency of its commission, and it is associated with the Forest in the same way as the Verderers, Common of Mast (which allows pigs to root for acorns and beech nuts during the pannage season), drifts, the use of 'furze' to mean gorse, etc. Students of law who come from anywhere near the Forest are invariably asked by their jocular dons if they intend 'to specialise in incest' and in some settlements everyone seems to have the same surname – witness the necessarily confusing cricket match reports in the *Salisbury Times & Journal*.

(c) In *The Secret Yoke* Philip Philips suggests that among the emotionally stunted and culturally bereft a father's intercourse with his daughter is a means of displaying affection that he is otherwise unable to communicate. Well, Wendy's father is dead so we can't wake him and ask him *why?* It would doubtless be a bit like the old one about God and theology; and, besides, conventional communication was beyond him – if he did that to his daughter what would he have done to an inquisitive stranger? He really was not good at talking. Getting any words, let alone the right ones, in the right order was a problem. The sort of sentence in which he exhibited the greatest verbal flair was something like: 'Wendy gonna come do ummagumma wi' Da then.' (*Ummagumma* is an onomatopoeic representation of the sound of heterosexual intercourse and was current many years before a pop group used it as a record title. In all likelihood there are special circumstances that account for such a coinage.)

(d) *There is always a tribe.* There is indeed. I give you the Karens of eastern Burma: their backs bear tattoos of the rising sun, their teeth are blackened, their children blow poison darts through foul pipes, their women's necks are stretched by brass coils, they worship bronze drums and use chicken bones as instruments of divination. Endogamy is their norm. The marriage of father to daughter is common and a man's daughter is often his grand-daughter; relations are scrambled and the population is stationary. The men of this tribe were not valued recruits to the Burma police. I give you too, from the happy head-hunting grounds of the East Indies, a gamut of peoples whose families would resist depiction on all but the most tortuously pleached genealogical trees.

(e) In the dark house of incest, heredity and environment meet laughing madly, swop clothes and forge abominable determinant irons from which there is no escape.

(f) The child of an incestuous union will often not achieve immunity to disease, may suffer a deterioration of the retina that causes blindness in middle age. The incidence of *total* colour blindness, albinism, ichthyosis aka fish-skin disease, alopecia and deaf-mutism is higher among such children than among those exogamously conceived. Further, anomalies may be progressively exaggerated – from here is the way forward to geeks and prodigies and monsters.

(g) What she did with her father did not contaminate the day-to-day stuff of her childlife. This is an instance of her gay bright girlish lightness: early one green morning when there was a frisky look in ponies' eyes Wendy met a group of worried boy scouts who had been sent to Dennis's shop to buy lard for their breakfast fry-up. At their camp they had bacon, eggs, sausages, bread, Primus stoves, methylated spirits, but no lard. And Dennis, though they could see him in the back room behind the shop grinning gleefully and tapping his thigh in exaltation, would not open up – he seemed so preoccupied that he did not hear their taps on the window. Taking her cue from her new friends Wendy does a good turn. In the kitchen there is a bowl of dripping (there is also what looks like a grey rubber mat beneath the stove – that's dripping too). But Bon is holding the bowl, dipping a crust in it. She dares not take it from him, and so, determined not to fail the scouts, she improvises. She gets an old chipped mug and goes into the bathroom where a brown thing partially covered in lustrous hair is bleeding beneath the dripping cold tap. The jar is empty. She goes into the room where she and her father stay. It is dark and damp and warm. She crawls across the felt-like blanket that he used to stuff into her mouth to quiet her and finds a new jar on the floor. She takes off the lid and bangs the bottom with the ball of her hand. There is a noise of a helpless creature being sucked into a bog; when the mug is half full she goes and offers it to the scouts who accept it with unalloyed gratitude. That night when Wendy is outside drawing the last breath from a chicken Wendy's father strikes Bon, causing him to cower on the floor where he kicks him and tells him he'll tan him proper if he ever steals his Brylcreem again.

Pigeons are doves who have fallen; foul and fast-breeding vectors of diseases that afflict men's lungs. What Dennis was so happy about that morning was that his deterrent to the dozen birds Wendy's father kept had worked better than he dared hope. On all the surfaces that they frequented and decorated with their limited repertoire of action daubs he had spread a thick, sticky gel designed to discourage them from landing. He had taken a lot of trouble, dancing parlously on ladders. 'He got out the skylight and crawled along the top of the roof. I couldn't bear to watch.'

He was well rewarded. A bird landed on Dennis's new fence and got trapped. No matter how vigorously it beat its wings it could not free its feet; it stood flapping determinedly like an exotic and verisimilar mechanical toy. Its petrol-blue crop swelled and its neck jerked and it made a noise that sounded just like a piping treble calling 'shop'. Then it started to bite through its legs. It pecked and pecked, first at one leg then at the other, bloodying its beak, balancing with ever less ease, going at it with what might have been mistaken for auto-fellationary rapture. The bird won. It flew off, leaving two ragged orange spikes on top of the fence and giving a new meaning to legless air-ace. To have maimed it thus must have given Dennis special pleasure for his own peg was giving him increasing trouble and he was getting to be known as Gimp. Wm and Bon called him Gimp and imitated his walk, left leg dragging behind, foot askew — theirs were really bad imitations (walking was not something Wm was too clever at anyway) but from the way they set about them it was clear that no flattery was involved.

Up at Stoney Cross ponies gather on hot summer days to bask in the heat reflected from the cracked runways of the old aerodrome. Beyond them is a backdrop of primary colours which resolves itself as you approach it into more caravans than you have ever seen in one place. Look at the O.S. one-inch 'Tourist Map' of the Forest — the Forest is on the O.S.'s doorstep so the information is probably correct — and you will see that the area round Stoney Cross is dense with symbols representing car parks, picnic sites, caravan sites, camp sites. (One Whitsun bank holiday 17,000 people camped in the Forest.) There is also, though unshown on the map, the *sine qua non* of an English day out, a large public lavatory in an apt cottage style. It was here that Dennis came on Sunday afternoons with the ice-cream van that he had bought for a song at a car auction and given a smart tosh of paint. The cooler wasn't that great and Dennis was, unwittingly, at the van of the soft ice-cream craze; when the weather got really hot the ice cream broke down and turned into what looked like chip oil with a sludgy deposit at the bottom. Still, business wasn't bad, though there were problems. The runways were popular with learner drivers and wildmen on large motorcycles who raced through the dizzy shimmer of July in self-soiled clothes. Also there was the clanging cacophony of the other vans' chimes and the radios everywhere and the cowboys from the dude ranches with their fringed shirts and monstrous snorting lather-covered horses and replica pistols and cheaply tooled saddles; these men made minatory whooping yodels and fired blank cartridges into the haze. It was here at Stoney Cross that Bon called Dennis Gimp to his face.

Bon had got to know some proto-hippies who had shown

him how to dry the caps of Amanita muscaria aka Fly Agaric, Tue Mouche, Divine Mushroom of Immortality, ambrosia, nectar, Soma. Bon liked to be blocked. He liked it more than anything in the world. Any salad of blue cheer, purple haze, strawberry fields, S.T.P., D.M.T., speed, browns, blues, hog, bombers, Do-Dos, Romala suited him fine, made him feel very good indeed. He thought the pictures that jumped in front of his eyes were wonderful, was impressed by every sensation that he experienced. The mycorrhizal (i.e. symbiotic) association that Amanita muscaria makes is with birch, more rarely with beech, unusually with conifers. It is the most seductive of fungi and along with Boletus edulis, in whose proximity it is often found, the most revered. It is to be found all over the Forest. Bon knew where to find it. He had found these at the edge of Bignell Wood at Brook, gleaming Jag-red jobs which *looked* unmistakably potent. He dried them in a low stove. It is impossible to gauge dosage. The cocktail of toxins that they contain is secreted by the kidneys and goes into the urine which may be drunk. There is no diminution of effect, though if the fungus is abundant and easily available there is no need to bother with such a practice which – sad paradox – relies upon the subject's remembering to and ability to fill a vessel whilst in a state of *advanced intoxication*. That is what the court called it.

The court also revealed that Bon had drunk scrumpy with coal gas bubbled through it. (This of course is a variation on the traditional Gorbals milk drink known as Backlands Bree which due to North Sea Gas is no longer readily available.) I suppose 'advanced intoxication' will have to do, but ... I mean, he arrived on the plain from the direction of King's Garn Gutter with no shirt, no shoes, just a pair of filthy trousers. Now he is on all fours, screaming Rampton screams and roaring; there are leaves and needles on his hair and his limbs are blood-beaded. Now he is on his feet with electric bolts of atropine bounding round his brain and his tongue trying to get free of its roots. It is a vertical cartoon of *grand mal*. He is out of control. His vision is really fucked, it is as bad as a vorticist's; it is not a question of getting things wrong

40

by doubles but by squares and cubes. He goes to lick the saline scum from a horse's flank (a banally atavistic action in these circumstances – his mouth is dry and he cannot swallow) and sees the horse and its bewildered rider multiply themselves before him. All the vans that all the Dennises are driving arrive with the chimes playing one perfectly synchronised version of 'Shut the Door, They're Coming In The Window' (the fact that there is no commensurate aural distortion must be the least of anyone's worries). Now, in a gesture that is to fix his future in the image of Dennis and of that moment, Bon limps in front of Dennis's van dragging his left leg with craven glee, yelling: 'Ya gimmy barster, ya gimmy barster. Ya greasy grocer, ya greasy grocer.' Bon thought it was someone else's leg that was run over. The cracking noise revived in Dennis some sort of bony memory. The witnesses all agreed that Bon had put himself in the van's path and they agreed that Dennis had not braked; one of the cowboys claimed that Dennis had actually accelerated – his testimony was given weight by the fact that when he wasn't a cowboy he was a driving instructor in Chandler's Ford.

Dennis was an inept defendant – all overfamiliarity and crested blazer. He said he tried to stop. He said his leg was slow to respond. He said that the envelopes, which the police would do nothing about, were surely a mitigation. Endorsement, £40, one month to pay. In a separate case heard at the same time Bon was bound over in the sum of £75 to keep the peace for a year. (There was recently a civil action brought by a woman in a nearby village against *her* next-door neighbour who had been sending entrails to her through the post. The county judge found for her, awarded her 50p damages and made her pay £500 costs.)

Irene attributed Wendy's increasing bulk to improved diet. She no longer suspected that Wendy's father fed them on the meat of stolen ponies. She assumed that the jobs Wm and Bon got when they left school allowed them all to eat better. They had jobs at Fawley and at several of the sites on the west of the Forest where oil-boring has been essayed (they find the stuff, but never in sufficient quantity for commercial exploitation). Wm worked briefly at Marchwood power station; they both worked on the construction of the M27 motorway. Putting up the thousands of signs that announce picnic areas, etc. was well paid and undemanding though the perks were nowhere near as copious as they had been on the motorway (where plant and materials had been in ample supply. There is evidence of this in many settlements near the northern perambulations of the Forest).

Irene was wrong. Wendy apparently told Ivor the art teacher what was the matter but after that she didn't go back to school. Irene was astonished one day to see Wendy thinner than she had ever been. 'She had her arms pressed to her sides, tense, as if it was cold. It wasn't.' Then she went away. She became a waitress, living in at a lorry drivers' stopover. Later she lived with a man who had a fruit-holding and she sold plums and berries from his roadside stall by an old brickworks; she was in constant fear of being stung in the throat by a wasp. Later still she was at Derby Road, not far from where she had stayed with the woman who was her mother. No doubt she wept when she recalled Bon with the adze and the dripping sheet coming back into the house. She was at Derby Road at the time when another girl was prosecuted for sitting naked in a front window – the girl got off, *she had not been moving*, though the verdict was reversed on appeal. From the last house she was at Wendy must have watched the building of the sweeping span across the river that replaced the old floating bridge.

There are many other things I could have told you about her and about the Forest: the rasping fires and the charred trees, the insurance arson at a lonely hotel, the dancing figures around nocturnal bonfires, the vipers on the heath, the parrot whose head was bitten off for a pub wager, the fact that Wendy's father and the woman who was Wendy's mother were ... Oh, the room is full of meat flies, I must go.

42

Filthy English

I can't tell an athlete's foot from an Achilles heel, I wasn't schooled by Scholl. Tell me a tarsal bone is a tool for dubbing boots, and I'll believe you. I have never suffered a verruca. I have never drunk champagne from a slipper. I have never had occasion to push my tuberous big toe (either of the sullen buggers) into an orifice owned by another person. The design of shoes does not interest me; so long as they're comfortable and watertight I'm happy to wear any style – Mother buys me a pair in the sales each January. The pedal fetishism of the magazines that Mr Patel displays on the top shelf, out of harm's way, seems to me comic – though not so comic as the quasi-synedochic use of 'harm's' to mean 'children's'. The Chinese practice of inhibiting growth with bindings does not appal me. My own left foot is misshapen as a result of the bombing raid on Southampton in which my father and sister died and I still get around all right; anyway, Mrs Tsui at the Jasmine Kitchen near the station has rather big feet. My attempt to look over the counter at them, twenty-two weeks ago – when I had just started on *foot*, was, I'm afraid, mistaken by Mr Tsui for a cockroach hunt. A comparative gape at one of Mother's shoes assures me that Mrs Tsui takes size 5½ or 6.

Fieldwork like this is not my usual practice. Day to day knowledge of the referent is no use to the lexicographer. As I say, you do not need to be a chiropodist to trace the etymology of plate or dew-beater or purp or cheesey anymore than you need have known a father's rough hug to trace boss or gaffer or trunchy (aka trunchie) — I was little more than two years old when he died and have no memory of him, or of poor Millie. I suppose I had already begun to call him Dada. I could, when I was working on *father*, have asked Mother what I called him but she has never really recovered, she doesn't like to talk about him. She is so liable to be upset by the slightest thing. Take, for instance, her reaction to a card that I received one morning from a regular correspondent, David Skinner of Manchester University: 'At last, Ian, a chance for you to immortalise your own name in your work! I take it you are still on foot, so to speak ... In a rather dreary novel called *The Port at Dawn* by Lewis Simpson (Robert Lord, 1944), on p. 138 one of the characters says: 'Have you ever seen them Joey? Blooming great spodes he's got. Some nights I lie there and think, tonight he'll leave his boots on and when I've gone to sleep he'll come to my doss and jump on me with those frigging spodes, jump all over my neck and face, Joey.' I think that as words for foot go it has some charm, and of course the fact that it's **your** name lends it something too. I'm sure the J.D.V.U. would love a piece called **Spode on Spode**. Yrs. D.S. P.S. Should the Reading Room not have a copy I'll requisition the one I read.'

Mother plumped the pillow behind her, put her newspaper on the tray and adjusted her bifocals — a gestural admonition of the handwriting of David Skinner and most of my correspondents (with Mother unclear handwriting is a *moral* failing). I expected her to be a bit tickled. She often is in the morning, by items in the newspaper. She wasn't. Indeed, she was quite upset. Her hurt anger was out of all proportion to the discovery that she was an eponym for foot. I removed the tray as requested, telling her quite sharply that she was lucky her name was not Barbara Hooker or Barbara Bastard or Barbara Brown. I'm afraid that she burst into tears and told me: 'If only you knew ... ' I could still hear her sobbing when I reached the bottom of the stairs. Very likely that card had prompted one of her periodical binges in which all sorts of regret (her forty-odd years' widowhood and unshared mourning, my choice of career, my failure to marry and 'carry on the name') combined to make her stay in bed for the day, summoning me through my study's ceiling with thumps on her floor. That day I fetched her tea, sherry, rice pudding, aspirins, multi-vitamin tablets, eight magazines (she likes to enter competitions), new batteries for the radio, two packets of rich tea, more sherry, a tin of fruit salad. I also established that there was a Reading Room copy of *The Port at Dawn* and did some valuable if unstartling work on *hoof*, the date of whose earliest occurrence I hope to push back to as early as 1550; I further hope to uncover an instance of *on the hoof* used in a cannibalistic context — that really would be a find. At about four o'clock when I went in to Mother she was thoroughly drunk and told me, as she always does in that state, that I am a bloodless bookworm, lacking in guts, that no one wants a forty-three-year-old who lives at home with his mother, that my father was a king.

Here is an idea so bad it should be trampled on, stamped underfoot. It is among the tired stock received and repeated by journalists, thinkers — people of that calibre. It is the idea that slang is born of secrecy, exclusivity, self-protection. The illustration invariably cited is that of the candlelit alehouse where the constable with his ear to the back of a settle cannot understand the conversation of two footpads sitting on it because the words they use are unknown to him. It might of course be a neon-bright bar or a bevelled-glass gin-palace and the constable might be a G Man or a peeler — the banal premise stays the same: our two ne'er-do-wells are able to

plan thefts and boast murderously at the tops of their voices in
the most public places. A likely tale. A tale to strain credulity.
It is a commonplace, anyway, that police and criminals,
hunter and quarry, speak a common argot ...

No; as I have convincingly argued in my papers in the
'Journal of Demotic and Vernacular Usage', slang is inutile
save in *the act of its creation* where it affords the speaker an
opportunity to display wit, lexical skill, ludic exuberance and
an overt attitude towards the referent. Thus the words that
possess the greatest synonymic attraction are those that
represent the objects of our most allegedly affecting emo-
tions – sex, money and so on. Take buggery: the variety of
reactions to this act is evinced in the extraordinary range and
richness of its synonyms. My own reaction, for instance, to
the thought of this practice is one of revulsion tempered by
bewilderment. I have no experience of it of course, but then I
suppose that many of those who have coined synonyms for it
are equally innocent of the actual action – verbal prowess
has nothing to do, I fear, with the red herring of 'experience'.
As a lexicographer I am evidently self-conscious (inhibited by
an *embarras du choix*) when it comes to choosing a slang term
that fits my feelings; moreover, Mother is most censorious of
both the subject and style of our conversation so I rarely have
any chance to try one out. My revulsion is specific and is
uncontaminated by base feelings of homophobia or by a
drear resentment that the meaning of 'gay' has been
irredeemably changed; my revulsion is of personal origin.
When the bomb fell I was trapped for several hours of which I
am fortunate to retain no memory and, as well as the injuries
to my foot that I have mentioned, I suffered damage to my
anal sphincter which a series of operations through my
childhood failed to correct; although there was no injury to
the spinal nerve that controls this valve the muscle itself was
badly torn. I am, consequently, prone to incontinence –
gimpy *and* runny, an improbable duo, no? I doubt if you can
imagine how irksome, how limiting this chronic condition
is, how fundamentally it has determined my life, how it has
diminished my social confidence. I am lucky of course to

have escaped the fate of Father and poor Millie and I try not
to feel too sorry for myself.

You surely understand, then, my feelings about buggery.
Riding the Hershey Highway is whimsical, colourful (both
graphic and chromatically apt), indicative of movement
though not of violence or pain; it is certainly inexpressive of
my abhorrence. It is an example of what in my paper, 'Slang
for Slang's Sake' (given at last year's Nottingham conference
and jocularly nicknamed 'Slang for Spode's Sake') I called
'radiant particularisation': brown (e.g. *The Brown Family*)
suggests, *inter alia*, chocolate (e.g. *Shoot the Chocolate
Speedway*) and chocolate suggests a number of brand names.
Thus we arrive at such synonyms as the one given above, and
Land on Mars, Rob the Dairy Box and at such variants as *Sue
Chard* (a generic term for passive male prostitutes), *Menier
Man* (a generic term for passive male prostitutes who also
offer 'French'), *After Eight* (a rich, sophisticated homosexual
trick requiring a passive catamite who can hold a knife and
fork properly. Its etymology is especially confusing since it is
also rhyming slang for date, rendezvous; and *after*, derived
from aft, was a naval ratings' word for doer and deed between
about 1870 and the Great War). *After* is curt and brutal
enough to express my sentiments, it does as well as *bowel
breaking* or *dung puncturing* and a lot better than mock
censorious formations like *bum banditry*, etc.

My initial hunch was that *spode* meaning foot was an
instance of 'radiant particularisation'. Josiah Spode was the
Staffordshire potter who perfected the production of calcined
bone china in the 1790s and whose company excelled in the
manufacture of ware bearing chinois designs. Plates of meat
= feet; Spode is a make of plate, and so on — by the
same process spode might have come to mean mate (in the
sense of pal) or fellatio. After reading *The Port at Dawn* it
occurred to me that I was wrong. Both the author and his
characters seemed lacking in the sort of fancy that informs
'radiant particularisation'; the book is a dour and, I

presumed, autobiographical account of the lives of a group of anti-aircraft gunners defending a port during the winter of 1940-1. There are flat quasi-technical descriptions of the recoil mechanisms of $3 \cdot 7$ inch guns, of loading procedures and emplacements; the characters are familiar ones — philandering corporal, nervous rooky, brutal sergeant, sensitive oddball, etc. They are believable and the slang they speak, though it is generically mixed (some of it is army, some of it regional, according to character), is authentic enough. *Spode* is the only neologism. I agreed with David Skinner; it is a dreary book, with the drab virtues of a documentary work. Nothing suggested that *spode* might have been an invention — I am necessarily wary of authors who invent slang for their characters. The late Dr Partridge, to whose Reading Room desk, K.1, I pay silent homage when I pass it, was often taken in by these pinchbeck argoticists. Not me. I spent a morning writing letters on the subject of *spode*.

My correspondent at Keele University, a former secretary of the Five Towns Dialect Society, had never heard the word. Nor had any of the Arnold Bennett specialists I consulted. Of the living novelists who have written about the Potteries, one did not reply and the other did so on a stained postcard with no stamp; he had not heard the word. These were the first in a succession of impasses. I was hampered by the author's tiresome failure to give the minor character, Nobby (who uses the word *spode*), a background, home, job before conscription, etc. Indeed Nobby is meagerly drawn, distinguished only by a fondness for reading out loud newspaper stories of carnage and crime, and by a chronic fear that the sergeant with the 'blooming great spodes' may attack him. Nobby's missing background was of moment because the word does not occur in any of the obvious places, e.g. dictionaries and glossaries of Second World War forces' slang or in the rare and precious booklets that give the jargon used by workers in the footware industry (I am grateful to the Northamptonshire Folklore Workshop at Rushden), by cobblers, bootblacks, footballers, dancers (Morris, ballroom, ballet), by chorus boys, hikers, athletes. The dismal fact was that it was almost certainly a nonce word, and one that was taking up far too much of my time; but try to imagine that it was *your* name. Try to imagine too what a surname, *sire*name, means to someone who didn't know his father. It is a bond with a past which, because it is imagined and dreamed, is an ideal, a past uncontaminated by a recollection of paternal rages, of beatings and ire, a past that is limpid and bright from pure invention. My name means a lot to me, more than yours to you maybe. So I persisted in my researches, though with no great conviction and with ever less hope of resolution after I learned that (Melvyn) Lewis Simpson, the author of *The Port at Dawn* and one other novel, had died in 1949 in a motor cycle accident. In all other respects my work on *foot* proceeded well enough. I took especial pride in my argument that *bludge* (mid-nineteenth century: Grain, Sheppey, Thanet) is an onomatopoeia from the sound of boots in estuarial mud, rather than a derivation from bludgeon — feet *do* do things other than kick people.

I received my good news the same day as Mother did hers. Brenda Church, a student of David Skinner's at Manchester (the one, evidently, who had introduced him to *The Port at Dawn*) wrote that Dr Skinner had told her of my difficulty with *spode*, hoped that the biographical information on the author she enclosed might help, gave me the address of the author's widow and informed me that she was completing a doctoral thesis entitled 'From Vivandière to Officer's Groundsheet: Hostile Representations of Women at War 1815–1945'. Melvyn Lewis Simpson, I read, was born at Downton in Wiltshire in 1916 where his father was foreman at a tannery. He was educated at Bishop Wordsworth's School, Salisbury which he left in 1933. For three years he worked as an office boy, copy-taker and cub reporter at the *Salisbury Journal*, New Canal, Salisbury. In 1936 or 7 he joined the staff of the *Southern Evening Echo*, Above Bar, Southampton. One evening in the autumn of 1937 Lewis Simpson, a tyro skater, fell at the feet of Peggy Barker in the centre of Southampton ice rink; they were married near the Itchen at St Mary's, South Stoneham, in June 1939. Lewis Simpson served in the Royal Engineers. His first story to be published, 'Bates Got Jankers', appeared in *Lilliput* in 1941 and is included in the collection, *The Gopwo Went Awol* (1944). He wrote two novels: *The Port at Dawn* (also 1944) and *Bailey's Bridge* (1947). After the war he worked for the B.B.C. and the *News Chronicle*. His widow's name and address were given as Mrs J. Milward, Fairways, Wellington Drive, Chilworth, Southampton. There was a firm thump on the ceiling. I feared Mother had fallen out of bed.

I met her on the landing. She was hurrying downstairs in her dressing gown waving one of the letters that I had taken into her with her tea and toast. 'I've won, I've won,' she said. 'I've won a *cruise*. Look!' She held the letter in front of me. Then she withdrew it and stared at it and shook her head in wonder. 'Remember that bottle of retsina?' I didn't. 'It was that one. That was the competition. I almost didn't buy it too. Twenty-one-day Greek Myths Cruise. Oh look — the birthplace of Zeus, Naxos, Mount Olympus, Delphi, Mount Cithaeron … Oh. It's *some* reward isn't it. Bring me up another cup of tea, there's my love.' I did so, and I didn't mention *my* good news for it would have seemed that I was merely trying to match her and console myself. Six weeks later when I saw her off at Gatwick on her flight to Athens I had already established that *spode* was not Wiltshire tanners' slang; further, I had had it confirmed that it was not used in the Royal Engineers. Mrs Milward thanked me for my interest in her 'first husband's' work; she wrote that though she was no literary scholar she was quite willing to talk to me, as she had been to Brenda Church and to a 'very learned instructor, as he called himself, from Brandice (sic) University'. She didn't know how much help she could be but was happy to do anything to perpetuate Lewis's name.

I traced Mother's progress on a map provided by the tour company. I had done the same when she had travelled in Moorish Spain, to the Cities of the Cathars, etc. The day that I set out to visit Mrs Milward, Mother was in Thebes which even in October would have been disagreeably hot for me. I went second class from Waterloo, well wrapped up and clutching my old brown briefcase. Although I was born there, at the Royal South Hants Hospital, I had never as an adult previously visited Southampton: the year the annual conference was held at the university there Mother had insisted that I accompany her to Lincoln, York, Fountains, Castle Howard, etc. – which I was only too willing to do since the ineffable Arminger was in the chair and would, I am sure, have managed to prevent me speaking. His only talent is for the manipulation of points of order; the man is a neo-nativist with an unshakeable belief in a crude, baby-talk connection between signifier and referent. Also, Southampton is without its own argot; it is difficult to think of a word that it has given to the common language. The taxi driver who drove me from the station to Chilworth could not think of a single one. Those words that he believed were peculiar to the place were migrants, or else common to all great ports.

It was a dark day and my natal city was dense with drizzle. Piles of brown leaves shone like well-buffed boots, cyclists teetered on the greasy streets, everyone looked down in the mouth, the windscreen wipers were ineffective, a blind man walked hand in hand with his little boy whom he'd never seen. We drove interminably through a murky avenue of great trees, past a bushy common and yellow brick villas, towards vehicles with their lights on at noon; then there were bright cheap shops, tawdry modern houses, blocks of flats. Beyond this, all rhododendrons and gravel, was Chilworth.

This is what Peggy Milward told me about *The Port at Dawn*, it isn't much:

In the spring of 1941 Lewis Simpson broke his leg in a regimental football game at Maidstone and six weeks later was granted convalescent leave. During the time he had spent in hospital he had written a number of stories (including 'Bates Got Jankers'); he resolved to use his leave to begin a novel. Though the characters in that novel were largely

51

based on men with whom he had spent the last year in the
Royal Engineers he set it in an artillery unit of anti-aircraft
gunners in the hope that his fellow soldiers would not
recognise their fictional analogues. At this time Lewis and
Peggy lived in a rented cottage at Netley; the sky above
Southampton and its suburbs was gleamy with barrage
balloons, at night it was bright with flak and fire. Peggy
worked as an auxiliary nurse. Among the soldiers manning a
gun emplacement at Weston was a local lad called Duffer
Clark whom Lewis had known during his time on the *Echo*.
He was – Peggy recalled – a bit of a ne'er do well, a Jack the
Lad; two-tone shoes and too much brilliantine, if you follow.
Good with engines though and quite a wit if you didn't mind
things a bit salty. During his leave Lewis spent a lot of time
with Duffer who, in exchange for drinks, gave Lewis all the
detailed information he needed for his novel. Lewis said
thank you, if you like, by putting him into the book as
Nobby. I am as sure as can be, she said, that *spode* must have
been a word he used; Lewis wouldn't have made up a thing
like that, he was a stickler for accuracy. I read all his books for
the first time in thirty years recently, the first time I'd read
them since I remarried and there so many little details I
recognise, all quite unaltered from the way they happened.
The last time I saw Duffer Clark was at Lewis's funeral – we
were living in London when it happened, I and Kit moved
back here afterwards; he came up to me, Duffer, and said, 'If
there's anything you want helping out with ... ' He had a
garage at Bursledon. You know I must have gone past it
enough times but I never stopped in. He died, oh, ten years
ago now. It sounded like cancer. I saw it in the paper.

   Peggy Milward gave me a late lunch and I told her about
my work whilst silently rueing the lost etymology of *spode*.
She telephoned for a taxi for me but the control couldn't say
how long it would be coming so she walked with me to the
bus stop. The afternoon already looked like dusk, the
rhododendron bushes were black and there was a fungal
smell in the damp air. I shook hands with Mrs Milward and
got on to a City Centre bus whose conductor called out the

approaching stops thus: 'Bassett Wood – that's Wood not
Hound ... Glen Eyre – that's Glen Eyre, not Fresh Air ...
Colony Road – last outpost of the Empire, and if you see
who lives there you'll get what I mean.'

Colony Road. That was where I had once lived, where I
just escaped death. Number 49, Colony Road. That address
appears twice on my birth certificate – as that of my father,
Lawrence Spode, Shipping Clerk, and as that of the inform-
ant to the Registrar, Lawrence Spode, no occupation given
this time. It was not nostalgia that prompted me to step down
from the bus on to the shining pavement; the objects of
nostalgia are things, homes, that one has known. I have only
known one home, that which Mother made for me after
Father and Millie died; homes one had before the age of
sentience don't count. The only memory I had of Colony
Road, indeed of my father, was something or other to do with
darkly dressed men coming into a room where I sat beneath a
table; the undertakers, I suppose, so it can't have been our
blitzed-out house in that case. I turned into Colony Road;
where, I wondered, are Father and Millie buried? What
would I now find occupying the site of Number 49? In this
road there were acacias and monkey-puzzle trees, privet and
cotoneaster hedges, houses with stern gables and bad-
tempered brickwork – red and black and grey. There were
turrets and spirelets and barge-boards – preposterous or
nightmarish according to the light. In this light they were
nightmarish. They grew more nightmarish the higher the
numbers got, as though representing the architect's climb
into a gothic psychosis: roofs rose from each other in apparent
defiance of gravity, tortured chimneys multiplied in vertiginous abandon, the fantasy grew ever more malevolent.
Number 45, Number 47, Number 49. 49? Where there
should have been a bare site or a newish block of glass and
concrete there was a house contemporary with all the others
in the road, a house that was more horrible than I can tell, a
house as strange as a sideshow freak from whose abdomen
protrude the lower limbs of his vestigial twin. I looked all
around me: the house was at a crossroads where Colony Road

was bisected by Boeotia Road. It occurred to me that (a) the house numbers in the road had been changed or (b) this was, by a numeral coincidence, 49 Boeotia Road. A quick recce round the corner ruled out (b). I returned to the front of the house, its number was newly and crudely painted on a stone gate pier, but above it, near the top of the pier there was still discernible the two figures, 4 and 9, that had been cut into it when the house was new. This house was, and always had been, 49 Colony Road. And, as if in confirmation, my bad foot began to hurt (from the damp doubtless) and I knelt to loosen my shoe laces; I tied a neat new bow and looked up at the house — my eyes were about two feet above the ground, at tots' height, and the place was, suddenly, utterly familiar. Its continued presence, its existence four decades after it had been struck by that bomb compromised *my* existence, it seemed like a refutation of my identity; yet the very fact that I was there on my haunches gaping at it showed that I was O.K., that I hadn't walked through the wall into another state. It did show that, didn't it? I'd have given anything to be able to telephone Mother.

'It's a most curious house is it not?' A man in a long black coat stood above me. His long face and bald pate were pale as bone, glowing and smooth. He held a packet of tea in his attenuated fingers.

'I was just … looking at it.' I stood up. He was older than his flat emphatic voice had suggested, his hair was dark, lank, dyed.

'The architect ended his days in Bedlam. That's not a fit fate for any man. You see, he gave you pleasure. His work drew you to it, you admired it.'

'Is this the only Colony Road in Southampton?'

'Yes.'

'And this house — it's always been Number 49?'

'Yes,' he said, 'this house has always been Number 49. I must be getting on.' He smiled and walked between the gate piers towards the front door of the house. He had almost reached the spiky wooden porch when he turned and held up his packet with a martial sort of gesture. 'Do you want a cup of tea before you go?' I nodded and walked towards him across the seedy overgrown drive, towards the twilit house where some windows had blankets instead of curtains. The screams of children came from high up in the gables. He held open the front door for me and I followed him along a drab tiled hall where unopened letters lay against the wainscot, and then down a flight of basement stairs. He unlocked the door at the bottom of the stairs and turned on a light. On the door was an electric bell press and beneath it was taped a card. The name E. HEPWORTH RAWLINGS was written on it. The room was chaotically furnished with a narrow bed, a chair, an armchair, a Baby Belling, a bulging bookcase, a wardrobe; on every surface were piled books and pamphlets. Through the window was a blank area wall, mapped by damp and cracks.

'It is,' I said echoically, 'a most curious house.'

'Yes, yes it is.' He smiled, his lips were engorged, mottled in gay membranous shades. 'People often stop to look at it. I – oh, oh I only rarely have visitors, I forget myself – *do* sit down. And can I offer you some cheese?' I sat on the edge of the armchair and he took from his pocket a paper bag with a halfbrick of cheese in it. Its rind was grey, sticky. He handed me a piece on a plate with a slice of bread. 'Do you know,' he asked, 'what this cheese is called?' I tasted it – it was strong and very smelly.

'I don't know it. Perhaps it should be called Frenchman's Foot,' I said.

'Ah yes – or Frenchman's Tongue.'

'I don't know,' I said, 'I've never tasted one.'

'My – you're a sharp one. It must be called something but of course the little gyppo or celt fellow – whatever he is – in the corner store knows nothing. He does not even know the names of the products he sells. What hope can there be for him – there is a right name for every thing on God's earth. One proper fitting name. You must agree.'

'I don't, as a matter of... It's my profession, you see – words, I...'

'Mine too, my friend. Have a cup of tea, there. We share a

profession then, almost – you have words, and I have The Word.' (The way he said that defies written representation, majuscules are a start.) 'I have given my life for The Word.' He indicated the piles of books and pamphlets, nearly all of them old, bedraggled; on the sill beside me there stood – I recollect only a few titles – *Jewish Sects and Parties in the Time of Christ*; *Die Sadduzaer*; *Post Exilic Prophets*; *The Words of Jesus*; *The Unwritten Sayings of Jesus*; *Die Stellung der Israeliten unter der Juden*; *The International Decline of Fertility in Political Arithmetic*; *Eine Antenne Direkt Zum Lieben Gott*. 'You would not expect to find such a fund of knowledge in a place like this. Would you? Did you have even the faintest inkling when you stopped to stare at this house? You can't have had.'

'Of course I didn't. I was surprised to find the house at all.'

'Come now. It's quite a landmark. The apogee of tectonic evil – that's a handsome phrase; but that's not what draws them here. You must know?'

'No. I'd never been here before today. I mean ... '

'An *innocent!* I shall tell you then. Once upon a time in this house there was a murder.'

The League for Christian Regeneration was founded in 1933. Its members believed in England, God and Adolf Hitler. H—— G—— (he is still alive, you can't be too careful), the heir to a Mancunian textile fortune, bought a small estate in north-west Hampshire near the village of Chute where a life of teetotal vegetarianism, prayer, poly-gamy, martial discipline and nudism was led by between twenty-three (in 1935) and nine (in September 1939) acolytes. Of the thirty-eight men and women who ever lived on a permanent basis at The Glory (as the house was called during the period of its infamy – it is now a preparatory school) thirty-two had been members of the British Union of Fascists; Oswald Mosley visited it in October 1934 and subsequently described it as 'a wen; they are ranting, mad and degenerate.' (Arthur Grant-Knox, *In Peace and War*, 1957.) Among those who lived there were: the architect Marshall Sisson, who designed a gymnasium (unbuilt); James Larrett Battersby, who in November 1945 paid £500 for a bust of Hitler that had stood in the former German Embassy in London; the Venn sisters, Laura and Marion, who in the 1950s formed the World Aryan Union and the Union of Aryan Motherhood; Lawrence Spode and Barbara Mary Johnson.

Rawlings continued: The majority of those who had lived at The Glory and all those who were living there when war with Germany was declared were interned under Regulation 18b. Despite having three times been arrested Spode was not interned, and nor was Johnson. (Spode's offences were (a) assault at a British Union of Fascists rally, (b) setting fire to a Jewish-owned haberdashery in Reading, (c) entering a church at Andover during evensong and yelling 'There is one eternal God — Adolf Hitler!') Spode, who often called himself the Reverend, and Johnson, who changed her name to Spode by deed poll, left The Glory in the spring of 1938, taking with them their daughter Magdalena (Millie); Barbara Johnson was pregnant again. They left against their will, expelled by H—— G—— because of Spode's apostasy: Spode and H—— G—— were agreed that the annihilation of the Jewish race and faith was a necessity. The latter deemed that this was so because Christ had been killed by Jews and there was an international Jewish conspiracy. Spode would hear none of this; he claimed it was a necessity because Hitler said it was, no more, no less, and that to give any other reason was a calumny on Hitler, an act of blasphemy. H—— G—— attempted to prevent them taking Magdalena, telling them that children were to be held in the common charge of the League in order to be taught, *inter alia*, domestic and racial science. Spode and Barbara Johnson resisted and they walked with their daughter to Andover where they caught a bus to Southampton.

He got a job with the Norddeutscher Lloyd shipping line and they rented three rooms at the top of 49 Colony Road. In

January 1939 Barbara Spode gave birth to a boy. She continued to bleach her daughter's hair. Spode found a better-paid position with Cunard-White Star where he was noted for his diligence and sobriety (Rawlings stressed this). He was also known for his abhorrence of swearing, of bad language and of loose talk — he threatened to put out the eyes of a fellow clerk who habitually said 'Blimey.' At night he printed and distributed leaflets announcing that Hitler was God's chosen son, that the swastika was God's symbol on earth, that world victory could only be had through the sacrifices of the Aryan martyrs, etc. Although he signed these Lawrence Spode, Hitlerite Missionary, he was never apprehended. After the outbreak of war he became more cautious and stopped signing them, though in other ways he was as rash as ever, waving torches in the blackout, telling his workmates that England should surrender, suggesting that Churchill was in the pay of the Devil (who was a Jew), that the war had really started with the foundation of the Bank of England which gave a licence to the gombeen-men of the usurocracy in 1694, that Hitler had been put on earth to scourge the earth of Rothschilds and Shylocks who promote wars in order to create vast debts on which they can extort the interest — thus when Hitler had won there would be no more wars since he would have erased their cause. And so on. On Sundays he spread a black and white and red cover across the mean dining table and conducted for his family a simplified form of the Hitlerian eucharist that he had conducted every day at The Glory — *Mein Kempf* and daggers and a broken cross were placed on the altar. If Magdalena tittered during the course of the service Spode would beat her afterwards; her injuries were on one occasion so severe that her parents kept her away from school all the following week.

On Adolf Hitler's fifty-second birthday, Sunday April 20, 1941, Lawrence and Barbara Spode went for an afternoon walk in the ruins of Southampton which had been recurrently bombed throughout the previous winter. They left Magdalena in charge of the baby. They looked at recent bomb sites in Portswood and St Denys and then rode on a tram to Palmerston Park where they admired the floral displays. They walked home up The Avenue, arriving at 49 Colony Road at about 4.15. As they ascended the stairs they heard a regular repetitive chanting coming from the top of the house. By the time they reached the last flight of stairs they could distinguish the voice as that of Magdalena. Lawrence Spode listened at the door before opening it very quietly. Kneeling on the floor with her back to him was Magdalena; the baby was beside her, transfixed. She held one of the daggers and was repeatedly stabbing a photograph of Hitler's face, chanting as she did: 'He is Satan, he's only got one ball, he is Satan, he's only got one ball.' There was nothing Barbara Spode could do to stop him. He kicked his daughter repeatedly for twenty minutes in order 'to make the devil leave her corrupt body'. After she lost consciousness the girl lay on the grey linoleum in her beige, leg o' mutton sleeved woolly and her father stamped on her until she was like 'a bird run over by a motor car'. He then attacked his son who had, he said, 'been irremediably contaminated by lies and filthy English'. He trampled on the little boy's foot and was, when the police arrived, attempting to sodomise him because 'Man is made in the image of God and Adolf Hitler and thus the most intimate communion that can be had with God and Adolf Hitler is through Man.' At Spode's trial much was made of the size of his feet (10½); he did not enter a defence and was deemed criminally insane. It was no doubt from a court report in the *Southern Evening Echo* that Duffer Clark picked up the name Spode and with delighted horror made it into his word for foot. Lawrence Spode entered Broadmoor on August 7, 1941, and was released twenty-three years later.

I left him lying there. His feet were indeed very large, and *broad*. He didn't look angry or frightened or anything, just very surprised. Who'll find him? I can't imagine he had many visitors. I think I inherited a capacity for strength in fury. Mother will be back soon, clutching her luggage and litres of spirits; in my hand I'll have my short arm, peter, porksword, mutton dagger, jigger, rod, pine, truncheon, log, dingus, beef bayonet, pecker, works, reamer, meat loofah ... I'll show her.

Spring and Fall

Have you ever tended a child's grave in winter? Do you know what it is to look down on the earth that covers the bones you made? Do you remember the smell of wet leafmeal? Did you feel the cold in your knees? Did you weep when you wiped the grime from the name on the tiny headstone? Did you think about the day you first came to this place? It was a long while back; it was a lifetime ago that we buried Jolly whose life was meant to extend beyond ours, not to be pathetically bracketed. The sky was dilute blue and bales of cloud rushed from the west. A boa of smoke blew across the crematorium's roof. Our nails bit each other's hand. Our eyes feared meeting. The path was striped with forsythia blossom. We picked our way between other little graves whose dereliction belied their epitaphs. We haven't forgotten you Jolly. Why did you *want* to join all those other little boys and girls? Why? We loved you Jolly. Every year we've celebrated your birthday; you'd be as old now as your mother was when you were born. I want to know what you'd look like. I want to know all about the man you would have been. Sometimes — pushing through the market, say, to old Morris's stall (though it's his balding son that runs it now) — sometimes I catch a face, a smile, a conjunction of cheek and eyebrow, something in the grin of a man in early middle age that tells me this is the way you'd be now. And I've seen your mother turn, her head hauled round by a voice she's heard, her eyes bright for a systole with recognition. And for long after you'd put this immeasurable distance between us I used to see her clear the vapour from the kitchen window and gape through the smeared pane at the empty garden. The photographs of you are just about surrounded by her buttonhooks now; it's quite a collection — ivory, mother of pearl, jet, Worcester, Limoges, so on. The photographs are browner than they were, mostly; but the one that shows you getting the cup for diving is as clear as the day we framed it and you pinched your thumb in the mitre.

We love you still. When you were very young every puddle was your lake and every stone that broke its surface was your island. The sun made the island the tip of an isthmus. It made the lake quicksand in which you dared not dip your finger (we watched you). It made the quicksand crazed, it made it your delta map; you gaped, haunched and absorbed. You had such a faculty for wonder — the worm of covetousness had not entered you then. You pressed your face to a Christmas window and turned to me with looping white breath all over your cheeks. It was delight that lit your face, not envy, not desire. A girl in furs squeezed between us with a crisp parcel. 'Isn't the bridge super, Daddy — it's just like Skew Bridge.' And you rubbed your gloved hands and your eyes granted you ownership (I want another word) of those exquisite, busy models in a way money never could have; I mean that your response to those electric and metal reductions of the real was chaste, that the delight you'd have taken in them had we brought them home would have been a shadow of your original delight that icy dark teatime. You regarded the world as an ideal salad of museum and cinema whose spectacle you relished with passionate quiescence. We should have warned you, shouldn't we, that there were far more terrible things in life than the swelling meniscus on a black tarn and sail-ships on a canal high above a fenland

62

road and the angry giant's roar of white water. Shame, hatred, despair – these are the terrible things I mean, the things that you suffered, that contaminated you. How could we have warned you? What could we have done? Why was it *you* Jolly that had to find those wicked people? Would it have made any difference if we had told you?

Jolyon was born during the second winter after the war. I held him in my arms and you held him to your breast and then you both fell into sleep and I trudged back home, across the frozen city where the ubiquity of icicles and the snowy sameness of the streets at dawn gave it a strangeness it hadn't had when, childless, I had passed that way the day before. Then there had been whining motors and skidding vehicles and people walking pigeon-toed, the way they will on ice. Now it was quiet. The whole world looked as if it was freshly hewn, newborn, as if the ideal that parents want to present to their children had actually come to be. It augurs well, I thought, and stamped my feet in a little dance on the packed snow. We had no more children (we weren't young). You suffered a breast abscess. The pipes froze and cracked, froze and cracked. Our son's nappies froze on the washing line like the leathery wings of primitive birds. It was a difficult time. He was, necessarily, a solitary little boy. The children of our friends were mostly ten years older than Jolly, and few children of his own age lived near by. When he started school he was disinclined to make friends, he seemed to have no need of them. He came everywhere we went. On the beach at Osmington Mills we ate rook pie and he collected wreaths of seaweed for us; from the bridge at Clifton he stared down into the Avon gorge while I explained how a Victorian suicide had been thwarted by the parachute effect of her hooped skirt; at Studland he made his sun-blistered, cochineal parents wait while with his beach spade he dug a grave for a naked, featherless baby bird that had fallen from the nest – he marked the place with a pinecone; in a drowsy garden, all hollyhocks and bees, he listened to an old lady's recollection of reading newspaper reports of Blondin at the Crystal Palace and prompted her with details when her

memory faded. He was a joy to us; the inevitable truncation
of his name belied him, he was really rather grave. He lived
in a garden with green hedges fat as clouds, he climbed hills
and walked on stilts and vaulted over walls.

High up there, four miles above this dismal heath – Hoch,
in East Friesland – was Alick Welch, masturbating.
Nineteen years old, shortish, rear turret gunner, cold,
morgue cold that mortally cold night, dimped Weight in his
lips, gloved, balaclav'd, dreaming of Annie, dreaming of
Annie's cellulitic thighs bulging beneath the pressure of
frayed suspenders that were flesh coloured (though not the
colour of Annie's flesh, *that* was grey like whale meat),
dreaming of all the tarts in Nottingham with their skirts above
their heads, of splayed pudenda, of ruched red anuses, of
Ruby the Red Rimmelled Rimmer, of Minnie the G.I. Bait
he'd have from behind. Tail-end Charlie. Two pairs of
uniform trousers and one of dun combinations were round
his knees. His half-bare bottom was on his parachute pack.
His Mae West sat clammy on his chest. His gloved glans beat
to a rhythm that when he got it right – and the flesh he saw
was potent, low, corrupt – overcame the concussing throb of
the engines. A lip of moon grinned doltishly at him; it was a
pig of a night – no cloud cover and fine visibility. He made
Annie hold a banana, now that really was rare fruit. The
aircraft banked a bit and his Thermos flask rolled against the
gun's plinth. The engines' ochreous glow was all bent wedges
and lines on the perspex panes of the turret's dome. He closed
his eyes in time to see Annie hide the banana. His arm
ached. He felt dizzy from coffee and benzedrine and exhaust
fumes. He bit on a strand of tarry shag. Ruby's tongue – a
proboscidean thing from a truss shop window – went after
Annie. A urethral itch made him squirm and tense himself,
and Ruby's tongue found the fruit (bigger than it had been).
Now, now, now – Ruby eased the banana free of its cache.
He heard a labial belch. He was nearly there. 'Welch – you
there? We've got company.' He grunted, 'Aye.' 'Look to it

man!' This was a shriek. 'Bandit — Welch!' Ruby had disappeared, evidently taking the banana. A dragon bat had taken
her place, it rushed at him from the moon. He heard the
jabbering clack of the top turret gun. He tried to depress the
pedal to turn the dome but his legs were crocked by the strides
down round his knees. He wriggled vainly to pull them up
over his detumescence. His foot hit the pedal and there was
an hydraulic jolt to port and his gauntlet cuff caught over the
electric trigger of one of the Brownings. He didn't fire a shot.
The wings of the Messerschmitt 101 (Uwe Zimmer, pilot) lit
up with a deadly heliography that caused the fuel-filled wings
of the Lancaster to light in their turn with bigger, stronger
flames that stretched with easy breaths from fuselage to tips
like the gay trimming on a dull dress. From within the craft
came the cooking noises of wrong electricity and the groans
of metal and the shrieks of men whose gongs would be
posthumous; it all shuddered and bounced and fizzed with
novelty effects. Alick Welch left. He pumped his turret
through ninety degrees. A man with a crude halo of flame on
his head jigged spastically towards him — Hughie the navi-
gator: he didn't get out. None of the others got out.

Alick Welch dropped blindly through invisible ice. The
receding plane split into flaring fractions according to the
laws of chance and fire — the charcoal skeleton of Jumbo the
bomb aimer ended up near a rusty trough in a field of thistles
and horses at Emden. Alick Welch landed long before he
did, though he knew little about his landing — when he
pulled the ripcord the parachute kicked and its harness kicked
too, struck hard his naked pubis. Semi-conscious, he floated
down with his thighs and bottom white against the night sky.
They found him beside a leat, bleeding and supine with his
parachute stretched over damp meadow like an imperfectly
sloughed skin. He had been there for six hours. During the
night he had watched pale eels slither over his legs; these
sanguivorous creatures had not availed themselves of the
deep wound (he fell on an old harrow) above his right knee
but they had left him scared as hell. He offered his captors
damp cigarettes, and while he stumbled between two of them

with his blue hands gripping their coarse uniform coats he watched the third kicking cowpats, jinking and smilingly reciting to him the names Hapgoot, Yack, Yames, Drake, Bastin.

After eight days in a cell at Leer he was driven in the back of an open truck to Oldenburg. There he was put on the first of a series of trains that took him across the flat, brown Prussian plain, an unvarying landscape of rotting willows and canals. He saw poor people, children in uniform, starving animals; he didn't see a single pretty girl. At Schwerin he changed trains just before dusk. This was the last town he was to see for two and a half years: it was like the others that he had passed through. The buildings were black, unrelieved by decoration, barrack-like. The streets were empty, lined with boarded-up shops, starred with wastepaper, broken furniture, old pans. Early the next morning, after a night in a siding, the train stopped at Warnemunde and he was led to a waiting van. The prisoner of war camp to which he was driven was near the village of Lich, close to the Baltic and the Bay of Lubeck, so close that it might have been set there to promote fantasies of seaborne escape. There was always someone burrowing in the sandy soil. Burrowing back to the womb of their Motherland: that is what Alick Welch said later, though it is a remark otherwise attributed too. Alick Welch never tried to escape. He knew that the England he had been sent from was not so different from the bleak Germany that he had just crossed; and he knew that he was not much more of a prisoner here than he had been there. He happily resigned himself to masturbation and the accumulation of wealth.

I was raking over the lawn at the back when Stella came out of the french windows and called that we had company; I could tell from the way she waited for me at the top of the rockery steps that whoever it was wasn't quite her sort. 'It's a chappy who says he was in the Stalag with you Jeff.' I followed her into the kitchen and told her to put on the kettle while I

spruced up a bit. 'He's got his lady friend with him,' she said.
He most certainly had. It was her I saw first, sitting on the
arm of an armchair, leafing through *Picture Post*. She was
quite a piece of homework, very expensively got up, very
much in the style. He had his back to me, looking out the
window and I didn't recognise him. And I still didn't
recognise him when he turned round. He'd always been a
cocky one mind you but he looked a real swell, very trimly
turned out – cuffs on his suit, astrakhan collared coat. And
he'd put on a spot of weight. Of course he was all smiles and
pats on the back. 'Snelly, my old chum, how you keeping,'
he said as though he'd been thinking about me every day. I
told him I was back with Burrells and well in line for
promotion and he squeezed my arm and said: 'That's the way
my chum.' He said that he was 'getting into the construction
lark'. It was always difficult to know what to believe with him,
he always had a lot to say for himself – when he arrived at the
camp he never stopped gabbing about shooting down two
Messerschmitts and trying to rescue his crew. A lot of the
younger ones were a bit like that – plenty of mouth. But he
took the biscuit. He got a D.F.C. She was different, his
fiancée – very quiet sort of girl. I said she was shy and Stella
said she was stuck-up; either way she must have been as hard
as nails, to have been able to sit there as though butter
wouldn't melt in her mouth. I was a bit mystified and so was
Stella. I'd never been particularly close to him and though
we'd all swapped addresses on the boat (we were shipped back
by way of Hull) I hardly expected to see him turn up like that
out of the blue after a year. I'd had the odd pint with Waggy
who lived at Warsash and Phil Blake had brought his wife
down for the weekend that the Arsenal was playing at
Fratton, but then Phil and I had been real mates. I hadn't
even kept up with Albie Craig even though he was only up
the road at Waterlooville. 'I didn't know', I said to him, 'that
you had connections in this neck of the woods. I always
thought of you as being more of a London fellow.' He replied
that he still was, that he was down here on business. I suppose
I should have twigged what kind of business would bring him

to Pompey on a Saturday afternoon. He waited till Stella had
gone to top up the pot and then he pulled out of his waistcoat
pocket — it was a double breasted one, and you didn't see too
many of them even then — he pulled out all these slips of
paper, different colours, some of them no bigger than bus
tickets, some of them torn off the corners of pages. Then he
puts them on the table and says: 'There's your I.O.U.s
Snelly. Twenty-one pound nine and sixpence it comes to.
You add it up if you want.' Well, I couldn't deny that they
were mine but, as I told him, 'A game's a game.' I picked over
them: the individual sums weren't that much. The biggest
was twelve and eight. The date on it was January 6, 1944,
that was the day before Stella's birthday and I must have been
feeling a bit down in the mouth. It was written on a triangle of
grey card with a word in the German style lettering on the
other side.

The first couple of months he was there it was just the
weekly pontoon school he ran — he liked to call it blackjack.
Van-tay — that's what they used to call it. Then he ran it
every night. He was very good, mind, about giving out *his*
I.O.U.s, but I don't know that many of us kept them; he kept
a record of them anyroad. After about six months he started
on the roulette. He made the wheel himself from a hubcap
and a bit of a broken boiler that he got off one of the
jerries — bribed him I shouldn't wonder. You don't need to
fix the wheel, the bank's always going to win in the long run.
His hut was packed, it was like Monte Carlo. He kept the
accounts and he had this fellow called Tony Gage to do the
croupier stuff. He was a right little weasel, Gage. Popularly
known as The Rotten Plum. They made quite a pair; very
much the dogsbody Gage was, did all the heaving and
carrying so to speak. Take the football. It was Gage who
marked out the pitch. He got the football into inter-hut
leagues, inter-hut knockouts and that so as to make more
games for him to take bets on — before he arrived it had just
been kickabouts with jackets to mark the goals. He got them
to give us proper posts. He was fly; he'd watch the chaps to see
who the good ones were and make his book accordingly.

Very fly. He'd have given you odds on the chances of X or Y making a successful escape, anything. Of course I couldn't pay him, even when he had deducted what he said he owed me it came to more than eighteen pound, and that was a month's wages getting on. (I'm sure he was straight about that; he wasn't to know whether or not I'd kept those I.O.U.s) He said that he understood the problem and that I could pay him by instalments. He said that he'd collect the first one on Monday because he'd still be in the area – he made that sound a bit of a threat somehow. When Stella came back in and saw all the I.O.U.s and found out what was going on she really set to, called him a guttersnipe, said that she'd call the police if he didn't get out of the house. We thought that had done the trick – he left without a word with Veronica Lake there trotting along beside him, and they got into this big car, light blue, an American job, a Packard I think, with a chauffeur. 'It seems', Stella said, 'as though there are some that have been foolish enough to pay him.' And she gave me such a look.

He showed up on the Monday. I got a tannoy while I was down at the warehouse to come up to the front office and there he was, bold as brass, chatting away to Mr Colin like an old pal. He was just as friendly as he had been when he arrived on Saturday and said that I wasn't to apologise for Stella, that he could see her point of view etcetera, and that he was only too willing to 'extend his terms', to give me longer to pay, and to 'communicate' with me at work so that there wouldn't be any cause for embarrassment. I must say he had it off pat. I told him where to get off and said I agreed a hundred per cent with everything Stella had said on Saturday – I had to keep my voice down because we were right outside Mr Edwin's office. He kept on putting his hand on my arm, then he suggested that we talk about it outside. So we went out where all the flowerbeds are and there was his dirty great car with a chauffeur sitting in it. And he put up a finger, I remember, like calling a waiter in the films and the chauffeur got out of the car and walked over to us. Well, I got the message then. He was about six foot eight and built like a khasi. 'This is my assistant' — that's what he called him, his assistant — 'my assistant, Mr Cruickshank. Mr Snell.' He stuck out a blooming great paw. He really towered over me and I'm not a little fellow. 'So you were in the R.A.F. with Mr Welch. Pleased to meet you. I'm more a naval man myself, more one for tradition and that.' Then he went back to the car. 'Top notch, he is, old Cruickers,' he said, 'a real sport. I say, Albie Craig was obviously *very* impressed by him. He has that effect. You ought to look up Albie, have a noggin. So — I'll be hearing from you *very* soon, won't I?' And he gave me a big smile and jumped in the car. He called to me as I was going back up the steps — I could hardly hear him over that engine: 'What's your fancy for the Derby Snelly? Tell you what, I'm having a flutter on Radiotherapy, quick looking runner it is. And I'm going to have a bit on Airborne — old time's sake, out of sentiment. You should too.' That was the last I saw of him. I paid him all right. How I paid him. I paid him every week for more than a year. I never told Stella, and when my promotion came through I kept it a secret from her for quite a while — that way I could send all my extra to him.

This is what happened to Tony Gage, The Rotten Plum. He jumped. You can still see the place where he landed. You can still seek out Old Abeson the florist to tell you about it. You can still stand in the street and tip back your head and gaze up at the white cubistic cliff of Chaumont Court, gaze up to the point where it meets the sky (which was grey like the horse then but is storybook blue today). You have to imagine the figure appearing there, the protracted moment of hesitation, the figure getting bigger and its scream getting louder, the frozen alarm on the ground, the way the figure shuts out the sky, the way it changes from quick to dead, from being to body, the people scuttling to it, the man who fetched the blanket, the abattoir ooze from the broken head, the dark pond. Old Abeson will tell you that while everyone else's eyes were on the pavement something made him look up and that

he saw a head peep over the parapet at the place where Gage
had dropped from. Forget it, the old boy's brain has been
stiffed for years, he's all sendem and bedwetting now, he's
brittle bone and tired organs that are waiting to have the light
turned out on them for good. Forget it, this is the story:

The 167th Derby Stakes, run over one and a half miles at
Epsom on Wednesday June 5, 1946, was won by Tommy
Lowrey on Airborne. (The trainer was Dick Perryman, the
owner J. E. Ferguson.) This colt, out of Precipitation by
Bouquet, had its dam's colouring and was the only grey in
the race. Also it was the only one of the seventeen runners to
have won over the Derby distance. Its form was, however,
otherwise dismal; thus it started the race as an outsider, at a
price of 50-1. A week before you could have got 100-1, and
when William Hill Ltd of Hill House, Park Lane, W.1
(GRO 4321) stopped taking ante-post bets at noon on
Monday June 3 (just about the time that Alick Welch and his
assistant Victor Cruickshank visited Jeff Snell at work), the
price was still 66-1. The explanation for the shortening of the
odds is simple. The Derby is supreme among those races that
attract bets from occasional punters who gamble with no
regard for form or even for the likelihood of success – they do
not expect to win. Their wagers are tokenistic, superstitious;
they might as well throw their money into fountains. They
trust to benign magic, to the tortoise beating the hare every
time – which it didn't: of the other, unreported, races they
ran the hare won the lot. Their choices are invariably
determined by horses' names. So in 1946 White Jacket was
backed by Billy Luff, a central London milkman, because he
habitually wore such a jacket, and, for the same reason, by
the chair attendant at the Princes Theatre. 'That's the way I
like my girls,' said a sailor who put ten shillings on Fast and
Fair (which was, anyway, expected to do well). Peter-
borough, another of the favourites, was heavily backed in the
east Midlands city whose name it bore. In Cardiff, Glasgow
and Clerkenwell bookmakers profited from the interest of
immigrant Italians in Neapolitan. But no horse in that
year – the first anniversary of V.E. Day was to be celebrated

on June 8 – had a name so potent in association and so fatidically glamorous as Airborne who measured forty-two inches from hip to hock and whose jockey's silks were viridian and pink. This was a name to excite martial nostalgia and quasi-patriotic loyalty – this was a name that might have been given the horse in memory of those who had died in the air; as it was it drew the support of those who had served and survived in the R.A.F., of a blinded pilot living in St Dunstan's at Rottingdean, of men of the airborne divisions and their wives and sweethearts, of those who owed their lives to billowing umbrellas, of those whose faces had been reconstructed from their rumps, of men to whom the 'angle of dangle' was not merely a genital measure in locker room joshing, of girls whose men had not come back, of girls who would bear bulge-babies and nickname them Sprogs. Moreover this was the first Derby at Epsom since 1939 (it was run at Newmarket during the war): here was the renewal of a tradition, of a national institution. It would have been a crime not to have had a flutter.

More people than ever before travelled to Epsom Downs that wet Wednesday. Alick Welch was not among them. Ever since he had landed awkwardly on Hoch Moor he had been prone to sciatica; an electric charge nipped down his left leg and he could hardly move. Persistent rain aggravated the condition. It had been a dreary May and this was to be the wettest June since the year he was born. The travelling hadn't helped. The Packard was better than the Alvis and that was better than the Wolseley and that was better than the train. He had covered thousands of miles, he never knew how many. 'Tastes ever so salty Al,' said Pammy, making a clucking noise and clutching his thigh, 'that'll be that hake you had.' 'Skate, it was. Skate. Not hake.' He rolled across the bed and stepped on to the carpet. He let out a little squeal and hopped on the spot, 'My leg. Oh Mother o' God it's bad. Ooh it's like having a knife in your back.' He pressed against the wall and Pammy massaged his coccyx to no avail. He hobbled to the window, pulled back the satin jacquard curtain and said: 'Don't know if it's such a day for a picnic

anyway. Ver' grey. We can always listen on the old radio.'
'Oh Al, my lovely frock ... ' 'You look nicer as you are.' She
wiggled like a temple dancer. 'But I really want to wear it.
Here – you'd better come away from that window or
someone will see you.' 'They'll just think it's a baby's arm. I
tell you what. We'll have our picnic here.' He limped
towards her, grinning. 'Taste,' she said, and kissed him.

Chaumont Court was designed by the architects Pocock
and Chad in 1938 and building was more or less finished at
the outbreak of war. It stands between Baker Street and
Edgware Road. It was requisitioned by the government early
in 1940. Alick Welch was granted a generous loan by a
banker whom he had met as a prisoner of war and he bought
the block in January 1946. He moved into one of the two
habitable flats (it had all been used as offices) and let the
other. Tony Gage and Victor Cruickshank lived in rooms
rudimentarily converted into quarters for round-the-clock
telephonists. There were builders everywhere. In a basement
storeroom whose key was found in Gage's pocket after his
death there were 37,560 clothing coupons, 21,592 lbs
corned beef, 11,021 lbs dripping, 608 cases apricot jam, 294
cases plum jam, 36 rounds ammunition, one revolver. (I
have been unable to discover how many jars of jam there
were to the case.) At the inquest into Gage's death (St
Marylebone Coroner's Court, June 20, 1946) Welch stated
that Gage had been 'a bit browned off with things lately'. And
Pamela Mary Tucker agreed: 'He hadn't been feeling himself, not his usual self at all.' Balance of mind. Forget it.

Pammy put on the red-on-blue dress and matching
peplum jacket Alick Welch had bought her in Bruton Street.
Then she played with her new hat a while. Then she walked
downstairs – she didn't trust the lifts – to Cruickshank's
room. He had a hangover and was reading a magazine called
Sea Sprite; beneath the picture of a girl with stretchmarks
unhappily clad in a two-piece bathing suit (not yet called a
bikini) it said: 'And when the sea washes away the mark
which her body has made in the sand, it is merely collecting
another autograph.' She told him they weren't going to the

73

Derby but to come and have lunch then listen to it on the wireless. He nodded, she teetered along the corridor to Gage's room, this was the first post-Venetian age of the platform sole. She tripped on lumps of plaster but kept her stride. 'You sure?' asked Gage. He was sitting on a stacking chair in grey underpants with the *Sporting Life* spread on a scuffed, ink-stained desk. 'Really?' The girl in Gage's bed had tiny, blackberry-button dugs. She looked ragged, over-fucked, underdouched. She looked incredulous, resentful, greedy as Pammy counted off £100 in pound notes. Gage shrugged: 'Well, if you're sure that's what he wants ... See you lunchtime then.' Pammy turned in the door, 'That's right. You don't need to make it too early mind.' Alick Welch drank little alcohol. He enjoyed seeing people get tight at his expense, making fools of themselves, speaking out of turn, getting maudlin and tough. When Gage and his girl Jeannie arrived Pammy was giggly and Cruickshank was drammed and garrulous. He was wearing his chauffeur's rig and she had on her new hat and Alick was in a morning suit stretched out on the sofa; on the floor was the hamper that they had intended to take to Epsom. There were mint green plastic plates everywhere and two empty champagne bottles stood on the mock-Adam lucite table. Cruickshank hooked a shoe beneath the hem of Jeannie's dress — it was crisp, new, pretty, and she looked a lot better than she had earlier. Cruickshank fell back in his chair (it was hardly big enough for him) and started to recite the names of some of his favourite guns. Alick Welch stared at the girl and said, 'You've got my slips then Tony?' He stuck out a hand. 'Downstairs Al. Left them downstairs for safe keeping.' 'Right you are Tony. 'Snot the same as an on-course punt but I've still got that feeling you know.' 'You got, frankly,' said Cruickshank at some point, 'as much chance with that carthorse as I got with Vivien Leigh.' Someone opened another bottle of champagne. Pammy put on a record of danceband music, The Squadronnaires very likely, and danced with Tony Gage. Jeannie sat on the arm of Cruick-shank's chair and asked: 'What's the difference between

Vivien Leigh and a bar of Kit-Kat?' Cruickshank chain-lit another cigar and put his big bruiser's hand in her lap: 'You tell me, love.' Jeannie addressed them all: 'You only get four fingers in a Kit-Kat.' Well they fell about, could have cried. 'Saucy. You got a saucy one there Tone,' said Alick Welch. Gage crouched over the hamper and his eyes bulged and his cheeks bulged with the fruitcake he had just greeded. 'Hope she's not too expensive to run Tone,' Alick winked at Jeannie. 'The saucy ones come expensive, like to see a bit of dinari for schmutter an' that Tone. Don't want to break the bank … Still, a man in your position Tony … Eh? Mean, I'll bet that little frock cost some blighter a bob or two.' He winked again and Gage coughed — a barking choker spraying crumbs all about. Later Jeannie put on Cruckshank's chauffeur-cap, put one foot on a chair and sang 'Java Jive'. Then Cruickshank stroked her arms and neck while she drank brandy from a bottle. Then Pammy tuned the radio and a full-fruit voice grew in volume and boomed from the limed oak cabinet. Alick Welch wriggled for comfort's sake. Tony Gage went on eating. He asked: 'How much longer?' As they cantered down to the start the horses began to cast weak shadows.

At half way Happy Knight led and Gage was still in with a shout. 'What about Radiotherapy?' he muttered but the commentator ignored him. The course was soaked, soft; the horse for it was a strong one, a trier, one with stamina and heart. Cruickshank held out his bulbous fist in front of Jeannie and mutely aspirated 'One … two … three … four,' releasing his fingers serially. She smiled and lay across him. 'And's Airborne, Airborne, the grey's coming fast.' It was a bad dream. Airborne took the lead about half a furlong from the finish. 'I got', said J. E. Ferguson, 'the thrill of my life. He charged down the hill like a real good 'un.' To Gage that charge must have taken a long while. He had time to ask again, 'Radiotherapy?' His fingernails were brown with rich cake. Pammy closed her eyes for luck. Jeannie gasped, and again. Alick Welch slapped the sofa: 'How d'you like it? How d'you like it then? What about that! That's what I call a tonic.

Five grand eh? They're not gonna be pleased when they see you come to collect are they Tone?' Pammy knelt beside him, kissing him and squealing. 'You gonna collect now Tone? There's a lad ... ' Gage stood and wiped his fingers on his trousers. He nodded. 'Yeh, I'll go now then Alick.' He hardly glanced at Jeannie nuzzling Cruickshank's chest and writhing. He shut the door behind him. I think he must have gone right past the window of that room but no one saw a thing; it wasn't till twenty minutes later that a police sergeant called Emerson with ginger eyelashes rang the bell. Jeannie was on all fours on the floor with the dress Gage had bought her all bunched up and with Cruickshank moving quite in concert behind her. So Pammy had to come from the study where she was helping Alick Welch with some figures in order to open the door.

You'll have seen the terrace. I expect it's different now. It was lovely then — wallflowers and herringbone brick and a sundial that I used to lie beside and dream. I used to lie there half asleep and listen to the buzzing. Everything used to shimmer in the heat, the whole garden was a mirage — the lawn going down to the lake, and the trim hedges and the colours that all mixed like a box of brand new crayons; oh and the scent, it was baked, and so sweet. The heat used to come up from the stones as if it had been stored there since the beginning of time. It was an Eden, there was a cedar of Lebanon by the lake. That was where he was when I first saw him. I thought it really was a mirage, I swear to you. I thought I was dreaming. I didn't believe my eyes.

That was what I used to dream about. I wanted a child. More than anything I wanted a child. We both wanted one. Al:ck wanted one as much as I did. He was very good about it, about my not being able to give him one; he was never bitter, though there were times when he used to stay in London for weeks on end but he wouldn't have been Alick unless he'd had a few girls about the place. And besides, I never told him *why*, I never let on, so I suppose you might say that I was

76

cheating him too. I was pregnant when we married. Marylebone Register Office January 21, 1947. So if we'd had a little boy he wouldn't have been that much younger than Jolly. It wasn't much of a do, nothing like the parties we used to throw at Tilworth: I'll never forget Vic Cruickshank saying that weren't we a bit old for a shotgun wedding. I miscarried at the end of February. Nursing home just round the corner in Weymouth Street. Alick sat up with me all night, cracking a few jokes to keep my spirits up. He saw it. He never said anything about it, he never let on that he'd seen it, but I knew somehow. It was like a little skinned rabbit in a white enamel bowl; they carried it out past him with a bloody cloth dripping over the edge. He was always busy on business the other times. You can hardly blame him. The condition is called Habitual Abortion. Twelve weeks, then phut. It was caused by an incompetent cervix – a very polite classification, and that was caused in turn by a youthful indiscretion. I had a pregnancy terminated in 1944. I suppose I was luckier than some, they haemorrhaged and died – it wasn't uncommon. I used to have nightmares about having given birth to the devil. I was haunted by deformed transparent things that bled and grew wings and tried to move but just wriggled on the spot. By the time we bought Tilworth I think we both knew that we weren't going to have children. We never said anything. That would be '52 – the day we first went there was the day the king died. The flag over the Close gate was lowered and we asked a chap filling up the car why. He told us and said: 'I'll bet his last words were "One last gasper." ' That didn't go down too well with Alick I can tell you. He once sacked an office boy who told a story about Princess Margaret getting sozzled – he was a great patriot. I'm sure if he'd lived he'd have been rewarded – a lot of them were, for helping to rebuild Britain.

What really decided him on Tilworth wasn't the house, or the grounds, or the views but the fact what was called the Middlesward was so big you could land a helicopter there right in front of the front door. It was his ambition even then to have a helicopter: he knew he'd have one one day. Flight was in his bones. It was a while before we moved in. Alick wanted to supervise everything himself, and it was about that time that ――― ――― a property consultant (of whom John Poulson said: 'He pulled the wool over my eyes') tipped him off that Building Licences were going to be removed, so he was very busy setting up things in preparation. Of course it paid off. Our first complete summer there – not just visiting to see how things were getting on and having a picnic – was '54. We had the Pakistani cricketers for the day when they were playing Hampshire. He was a keen sportsman, Alick, he knew them all – Don Cockell, Keith Miller, Brian London, Randy Turpin, Freddie Mills, Denis Compton. Jolly loved to listen to him telling him about his friends in the sporting world; he wasn't so interested in showbusiness celebrities, he didn't really want to hear about them.

We'd had a spot of trouble to start with from the local children. During the years the house had been empty they'd got used to coming into the grounds. They were quite a rough lot, with thick accents, dressed in hand-me-downs. Alick didn't want to make trouble, and so he bought a donkey. That was quite a stroke; when they climbed over the wall – they always came in that side, from the village – they found Bingo there and played with him rather than coming up to the house. They weren't at all the sort of children that I wanted. No, they weren't my dream babies. There's always something a bit cheap about black plimsolls with no socks, and that's what they all used to wear. That's why we didn't adopt – you don't know what you're getting, you don't know what they're going to turn into. At least with your own I suppose you've got only yourselves to blame. Jolly was different. That was quite clear. He had my colouring *exactly*. Gold and molten gold. I looked up from my book – I think it was A *Summer Place* – and there he was. It was like a dream, as I said. I felt I was looking at a part of me. It was like seeing a version of oneself. It was as if one of those children I had lost had not died, as if he had been taken off and had grown up without me and had now come to see me. I actually thought that and I tried to work out where he could have been all that time. The whole while he was stalking along the edge of the lake where the bottom lawn was a bit brown with cedar needles. He had a white sun hat behind his back and tried to catch a butterfly with it; he lunged after the butterfly and stumbled then he stood up and beat his knees clean with the hat and then he saw me watching him. He can only have seen my face and shoulders over the edge of the terrace; he paused a second then pointed up at where the butterfly had fluttered off to, to let me know what he was doing there. It was such a sweet gesture, it was as if he was ticking himself off for having failed to catch it. I yelled 'Hard luck', and he must have just heard because he shrugged. I asked him if he wanted a glass of orange juice and he ran up the slope of the lawn towards me. His legs were quite brown, and so was his face: the sun had bleached the down on it, I could see the pattern of the down on his cheeks. There was a graze on one shin and the skin round it was a mite duller, not so smooth as the rest. I said: 'You won't catch many with that.' And he said 'It doesn't really matter. It was an Orange Tip. I'll get one sooner or later. Do you live here? It must be nice to live in a house like this. I'd love to live in a house like this.' He had stopped at the top of the steps up on to the terrace. I couldn't help staring at him. He was the most beautiful little boy I'd ever seen. I wanted him. That afternoon I took him out in the XK 140. He said it was the most super car he'd ever been in but he thought white-wall tyres were a bit sissy. (I had them changed that week.) Then we went to a sports shop near the Infirmary and I bought him a butterfly net.

Then his mother, whose hair the colour of an old tarnished florin was strained back so tight and straight across her skull that I wondered if it hurt, told us to go upstairs and wash our hands. The dark, tiled bathroom smelled of Coal Tar soap. On a varnished dresser there rested jaundiced bonehandled brushes, a chipped and repaired china wash bowl, a perished strop. He scrubbed his hands with a wooden nail-brush and then with a crouching mouse of pumice. I put my hands

beneath the cold tap and wiped them dry on my shorts. He
stood in front of his mother so that she might inspect his
hands. Then she inspected mine and saw the black traces of
the cricket bat's handle on the palms and told me to go and
'do better'. When I sat at the lunch table his father said, not
sharply, 'Grace hasn't been said yet Jonathan.' He looked
straight ahead of him through the window as though he
could see the Lord, whom he was asking to bless the cold
lamb and mashed potato, lurking beside the shaggy monkey
puzzle. There were also rusks, loaf ends dipped in milk and
dried in a slow oven; I was unable to eat them without loud
scrunching. I kept my head down. The meat was fatty,
fibrous, *fade* and I picked at it with Mrs Good, straight-
backed and masticating, watching my every move. I feigned
interest in a commonplace, cutglass salt-cellar. 'I think
Jonathan's French holiday has spoiled him for our plainer
food,' she said. '*Mummy!*' said Jolly. 'He's just a slow eater.'
'Their ingredients, French produce,' she said, introducing
me to the institutionalised lie, 'are very inferior. *That* is why
they cook like that. I'm sure' – here she tapped me with her
angular hand – 'you'll grow out of it soon enough.' 'We're
different from the French', said Mr Good, 'in climate and
geology, geographically, morally, spiritually. We should
thank our Maker for that, for making us different.' After
lunch – the pudding was rice and stewed fruit – we were
sent upstairs to Jolly's room to rest for half an hour. It was a
tiny, neat, meagrely furnished room, distempered a dull
buff. There were old editions of books by Richard Jefferies,
Hudson, Kipling, Haggard. There was a shelf full of worn
textbooks and popular histories, a framed and faded colour
print of Millais's *Boyhood of Raleigh*, another print, of La
Thangue's *The Man With the Scythe*, the twenty-third psalm
in needlework on a dun background, two Coronation mugs,
a rank on the mantelpiece of lead soldiers whose paint was
attrited with many lone waged campaigns. In a fabric-
covered chest in the window bay were the blocky wooden toys
of early childhood, a threadbare Teddy and limp soft duck
from earlier still, a clockwork railway engine and its small

80

oval of track neatly boxed. In an ancient cabinet with sliding trays were Jolly's dead uncle Annesley's birds' eggs, most of them brown and blotchy (sparrows, chaffinches) which made him a dull stick I thought; his smaller collection of impaled butterflies and moths also evinced a distaste for gaudy species. 'Look at this,' said Jolly who was crouching in a corner of the room with a contorted metal coathanger in his hands; he forced up a loose floorboard and lifted from its cache a blue and yellow box, then he crept out on to the landing to check the whereabouts of his parents. He knelt in the centre of the room, lifted the box-lid and removed from its litter of tissue paper a powder blue plastic model of a Jaguar XK 140 which he held up and surveyed with something the far side admiration. He put it on the carpet and switched on its battery-motor by depressing the 'gear-lever'; it moved towards me whirring, arcing because of the carpet's pile and Jolly followed it on his knees. 'Don't you think it's smashing?' he asked and I replied that my Triumph TR2 in the same series was British Racing Green, i.e. *better*. Without warning and with a tearful glare he punched my chest. The car collided with a bed-leg, turning on its side with its rear wheels racing like an impotent wounded insect; I made to pick it up and he seized it, hissing 'Mits off, Meades.' There were footsteps on the landing. Jolly pushed the car under the bed and put its box in the little wardrobe. His father's head appeared between door and jamb: 'If you chaps are still thinking of going bicycling you should be off soon — what's that?' The creased tissue paper billowed across the floor with the draught from the door. 'Jolyon?' Jolly gaped mutely at his father. I said: 'It's mine Sir. I found it in my pocket.' 'Ah. Well fold it up like a good chap and put it away — you never know when your mother may need it. Now, the forecast's for rain later so don't go beyond Dinton, and make sure you've got your capes.' Jolly clasped me on the shoulder, 'That was damned decent of you.' He replaced the car in its box: 'You see Pamela gave it me and my father and mother don't know about her. She's super, Pamela. Would you like to meet her?'

81

Jolly's rolled buttercup cape bobbed behind his saddle and I followed. Mrs Good, with a hoe in her hand, had scrutinised our road crossing from the garden and watched us as we pedalled out of sight towards Dinton between green banks fogged with cow parsnip. But just past the Nadder Valley Café Jolly turned off the road down a track thick with cowpats towards the river, which we crossed on a creaky wooden bridge. We carried our cycles across a tufty, thistly meadow till we came to the Bulbridge road. I followed. I guess that his keenness to see Pamela made him tireless; he stood to pedal up the steep beech tunnel where on those sunny days the light was the green that greets the pod pea. I got off and pushed; at the top he was waiting for me and we freewheeled down the dusty road into the valley. We followed the river and watercress beds for a while, then went past a group of council houses and proud-gardened bungalows, then arrived at a T-junction. In front of us was a brick and knapped flint wall with a thatched top; it stretched away as far as one could see in both directions. Of course it has gone now, the entire village is different now.

Pamela Welch does not remember my coming there with Jolly. She doesn't remember my standing awkwardly with my legs astride the cross bar while she hugged Jolly and his bicycle lay gawkily on the gravel. She doesn't remember my awe as I walked round the outside of the house, which seemed to transform itself from one house into another, which seemed to be in perpetual elision, which – such was its rapturous congruity with its gardens – seemed a place made in a dream. She doesn't remember – but then why should she? She was engrossed: as she stooped to pick a scale of dry lichen or something from his hair I asked her how old the house was. She didn't hear me, she was nuzzling him and her hair fell over his. She was a real bottle-blonde and nature had faked that for him so they looked kindred. She seemed to have so much to say to Jolly; I trailed behind them hardly catching a word. Her voice was charm-school cute, husky and flirtatiously mocking. She wore a tightish turquoise sundress that emphasised her tan. Her costume jewellery was abundant, of 'African' inspiration, and clacked and tapped racily. On the self-striped lawn that ended at the lake she kicked off her high-heeled sandals and ran; Jolly chased without bidding, whooping like a wardancer, and they dodged through the rainbow of a sprinkler. Later I sat beside the lake while Jolly raced up and down in a sleek blue kayak and Pamela timed each sprint, counting just out loud and running along the far bank. 'D'you want a go?' asked Jolly; his hair was stuck to his forehead and he was puffed. I eased myself into the tight cockpit and paddled gingerly, too gingerly – speed is what stops such craft keeling, this was one that was liable to tip either way. It tipped port, and I managed to prevent it going all the way over by jamming the paddle into the bubbly pungent mud at the water's edge. I called for help, and looked up and saw Jolly was waiting as Pamela put on her shoes. Then they walked up towards the house and I got soaked and mud-covered getting on to the bank. When I found them they were having tea – Earl Grey and sybaritically crustless egg sandwiches – in an airy, galleried room strewn with bright gewgaws in the Contemporary taste. Pamela laughed when she saw me: 'Oh dear Jeremy whatever happened to you … I don't think you can be quite such a sailor as Jolly. You'd better go and find Sandra and tell her to show you where to clean up.' I walked squelchingly to the pillared hall and then turned to ask where Sandra was. They were giggling together; Jolly saw me, he stared at me a second with disdain – it was something I knew, even at that age, I could never mention to him. After tea they splashed about in the pool. I, a non-swimmer, kicked a beach ball along the side. I had rather earnestly warned them of the dangers of swimming so soon after eating. Pamela – by now she was wearing a black one-piece bathing costume, a black straw hat and black mules – turned round to me as we walked down the arbour towards the pool and said: 'God you sound like somebody's mother.'

I saw her three more times:

(a) Another Saturday, later in the year, certainly after the Michaelmas term had started, I was with my mother in a labyrinthine shop whose shelves were loaded with Dinky toys and plastic construction kits and little tins of Humbrol paint and OO scale rolling stock in the old regional liveries. She stood at a counter beneath whose glass surface an entire vehicular world was aped; beside her was the man on whom I base my conception of Alick Welch. I take it that this man was her husband. He was small, got up in opulent weekend style (loud checks, lots of canary yellow, shocking orange suede brogues, a bow-tie), had a tan as pronounced as hers — to my child's eyes he looked like a foreigner dressed as an Englishman. They turned from the counter, both of them bearing several parcels. She beamed at me from within folds of fur and exclaimed: 'Jer ... Jonathan — what a lovely surprise ... ' She was bigger, blonder, glossier than before '... you *must* come and see us again soon. Tell Jolly I told you. So long.' And she made a *moue* and he raised his snappily-cut Lincoln green trilby to my mother who paused a second and asked with an incredulous laugh: 'Jonty — who on earth was that?'

'Alick Welch,' said my father, pulling off a pair of Wellingtons, 'is *a chulahka*, a wide boy with airs.' 'And she looks like Miss Fluck's loose sister,' said my mother to whom that filmstar's real name was a source of yet incomprehensible hilarity.

(b) There was an intimation of dusk at three o'clock and the tan egg made an arc from Jolly's foot to the long grass around a creosoted hut. Bulky with three pullovers I ran past the groups of boys in dark macintoshes to the place where the spiralling kick had crossed the white line. As I reached the spot I held up the flag and Pamela Welch, over whose head the ball had passed, said: 'It went out much further down. *Go on*, he kicked it down there.' And she tugged at the sleeve of my outermost pullover and trotted towards the goal-line. I stood ten yards beyond where the ball had gone out of play with my flag stiff in the wind. 'That's right, Jonathan,' she said, 'he's a big kicker, Jolly.' Throughout the game she urged me to exaggerate the length of Jolly's frequent kicks from what we then called standoff half: (before the emenda-

tion of the Rugby Union's rules a kick to touch from any part
of the field was permissible). Afterwards, as we walked
towards the changing rooms, a scarlet-faced man in a British
Warm (a parent of one of the defeated home team? one of
their masters?), caught up with me and tapped me on the
shoulder: 'That was a pretty sickening display I'd say. You
might think it's smart, I call it cheating. You should be
ashamed. Your school should be ashamed. What's your
name, boy – Your headmaster's going to hear about this
Meades. There's no place in a good school for a boy who
cheats.' Jolly, streaked with clay stains, said: 'We'd have won
anyway though wouldn't we, Sir? We didn't need to have
him doing that.'

Later, when Jolly asked me to look after his kit because he
was going home with Pamela rather than in the team bus I
agreed to. Also, I promised that if necessary I would cor-
roborate to Mr Bealing his story that Pamela was his cousin. I
watched through the Venetian window of the room where we
were to sit down to cocoa and bread piled high with sandwich
spread; I watched the rear lights of the Jaguar, coloured
lavender by the dusk, close on up to each other and disappear.

(c) The last time I saw her (before that day in San Luis de
Sabinillas) was early in the summer after Jolly died, perhaps
eight weeks after that horrible night. The Jaguar was at the
gates of the cemetery and she sat at the wheel, with the hood
down, wearing dark glasses and waiting to turn out on to the
busy road. I was in the backseat of my parents' car and I was
too embarrassed to draw attention to her.

I missed Jolly; for a while I cried for myself, later he was
rarely in my thoughts; I have learned that children suffer a
protective amnesia or at least develop a hide of forgetfulness.
And after so many years he seems no more dead than those
other childhood friends who have disappeared (disparaître =
pass away), who have adopted new identities in the backlands
of the world, who now wear the stern harried face of
adulthood. I'll never see them again either. Though when I
go back I look down the roads where they used to live in

case they too are revisiting the site of their former life.

Like attracts like. You draw to yourself the ones who would be you. We're all like mirrors. Love is impossible between those who aren't kindred. Vanity is the root of friendship. An ideal world is populated by models of oneself. Give to others what you want yourself. And remember, such reflective liaisons are conspiratorial. They are founded on the mutual recognition of frailties, on the fearful knowledge of the precise spot to press the finger that paralyses. These are the things Alick Welch believed, and I'd never dispute them. He lived up to his own precepts. Or he made up precepts from the way he lived.

(Vic Cruickshank does not really sound like that. He sounds like a man with an ox's tongue in his mouth. He suffered badly in Alick Welch's fatal helicopter accident: brain — nasty damage. He's lucky to be alive. But he can still nod in affirmation. And he can tell one lap rug from another. This one is Hunting Stuart.) He sounds like this, but *very slowly*:

That boy took Alick. Maybe that's what Alick wanted. He must have seen that the boy would take him. He was in a vile mood — the old A30 was chock-full of grockles off to Devon, and it was hot and muggy and Alick kept telling me to turn off and take back roads that led nowhere. It took three hours to get down there and I could tell he was spoiling for a fight with Pammy, I could tell when we went up the drive — he was looking for the blade of grass the mower had missed. I put the Roller in the stables, had a shower and a gin or three, and walked over to the house expecting to hear them screaming and all the little tarts in the kitchen giggling. Not a venus's. I'd seen Alick like that before, but never with a child. The boy had been teaching Pammy to play chess — some hope; and now he was telling Alick about a Spanish castle builder, someone Lopez: there was nothing he didn't know. It was like sparring, trying each other out. Alick liked that. Flirting was raw meat to him. They were way beyond the masons'

handshake. They both *knew*. They had each other's measure
and it came to the same, down to the last sixteenth. All the
boy didn't have was Alick's bad back. Otherwise he was a
bonsai-Alick. He'd even have got Alick's taste for tail.
Another thing he'd have got was Alick's generosity. She
mentioned the donkey for the village kids? Alick gave to
charity. His epitaph ought to have been 'He tipped well.' He
did, munificently. (Like Sir Eric Miller.) As it was *he* was a
grasping little quim — Alick wouldn't have been the man he
was if he hadn't seen that. *But he liked it,* he was a seam of
gold the boy had found and was going to stick to. Alick
enjoyed the flattery, the attention he got from him. Alick
used to fear that people didn't take him at his own estimation.
The boy saw him as he wanted to be seen, confirmed his idea
of himself, enhanced it even — by acting like the heir to the
manor. He was a calculating little so and so: he knew where
he stood with both of them. He *played* them, the way a cat
does. And they were grateful, really were. What *he* liked was
the way they showed they were grateful — trains, a bike, a
water *rifle,* an air gun, Dinkies by the dozen, a crystal set.
The room at the top of the tower was like Hamley's warehouse; the whore's vault ... the longer he stuck around the
more they piled on him. It was a disease.

  I'd never thought about his parents till that night. I'd never
thought about where he came from. He had the sort of accent
Alick had had to *remember* to do for years; I reckoned his
people must be the sort of nobs that don't give a
damn — that's what I'd have thought if I'd thought about it.
Those are the sort of parents he must have wanted — something like Alick and Pammy. They must have been like
make-believe parents come to life, glamorous, ideal, *young.*
The boy's Mum and Dad were old; old and dowdy. I hadn't a
clue who they were. You don't expect *anyone* to be hammer-
ing on the door at two a.m. on a freezing cold night. We were
listening to a fight on the radio — Patterson and Ingemar
Johansson, it might have been, I can't recall. America,
anyway. There were a few of us — the house was often full at
weekends. There was Fisk from Building and Public Works

and his bit; there was Jimmy McParland, shadow boxing along with the commentary — he was a great fighter when he didn't have to go in the ring; there was a bender called Halloran who was big in poured concrete and used to come for the shooting whatever the season — he was Alick's beard, he used to come with whatever bit of fluff Alick was dingdonging. But during the time the boy was around Alick stuck to the straight and narrow; the boy made him and Pammy like they had been at the beginning. He didn't so much as wink at a bit of twitch; afterwards of course it was all downhill. Who else? Pammy's friend Maxine who married this fellow that got sent down for currency offences — she wasn't married then. Forrester Jones, the nylon bedding man, he was in quilted tiles then. I think that was the lot.

There was this banging on the door and Alick told me to go and have a look. I undid the bolts and there were these two done up in old overcoats and shivering in the porch. He stepped forward before I could stop him and said: 'I believe our son is in this house.' I told him he was mistaken. 'Mr Welch,' he said, 'I intend to take him home. Furthermore I shall forbid him from coming here ever again.' Those were his very words. 'I'm not Mr Welch,' I told him. I was a bit foxed; they meant business. 'Will you fetch him in that case,' he said. I didn't have to. I didn't like their tone, I told them to scarper. I must have raised my voice a bit — I could be very loud, and Alick came out of the lounge to see what was up, and the boy came out just beside him. He stood at the end of that huge hall in his pyjamas and a monogrammed dressing gown, silk, that Pammy had had made for him. He was half asleep — he'd only stayed up to please Alick — but when he saw them he bolted. Up the stairs without looking behind him. She screeched 'Jolyon' and went after him. Then Pammy and Maxine came into the hall. You could hear their feet on the stairs. And when the boy got to the second landing he looked over the banisters. He looked like a frightened goat, white. He scuttled off down a corridor.

❧

88

That beautiful boy, my only child, my pride and comfort, the being that bloomed from the seed I was host to, the one that gurgled with ecstatic mirth, the one that tugged me and had me skip beside him, who leaped from walls sure as the seasons that I would catch him, that beautiful boy grew dour and silent. As winter came on and I tied his scarf and patted its knot and kissed his cheek his eyes stayed down, fixed deep below the frosty doorstep, and his mouth twisted into a petulant bracket. He toyed with his food, left his greens, detected gristle where there was none, was prodigal with butter, smuggled crusts from the table. He was by turn fractious and stiffly deferential (as he had been with your severe old Aunt May – it pained me to see him like that towards us). Whereas he had formerly been solemnly loquacious ('Hesmondhalgh says that there's sure to be war between Russia and China because ... Pondy doesn't bowl, he *chucks* like Meckiff ... ') now he would return from school scuffing the conker blossom off his toe-caps and ask why we did not have a television set. At weekends he would ask why we didn't have a car. He spoke to slight us with the inventory of his friends' toys. He told us the firedogs were old-fashioned, that Aga – the invention of a Nobel winner – was the best sort of cooker, that everyone had been abroad in the summer, that everyone had taken advantage of the relaxation in uniform rules and was wearing slip-on shoes, that property shares were the ones to buy, that Jonathan never had to go to church. He told us much much more in a spirit of resentful provocation. Of course we never told him that had the one bet that I had in my life not been successful he would be at the council school where he'd not learn such extravagant airs, that wouldn't have been fair. (I was queer, pregnant, tearful at the time I made that bet. I did it as a sort of homage in memory of my marvellous little brother Annesley who was shot down over northern Germany and was awarded a posthumous D.F.C. He loved the races despite our father's proscription. Jolyon looked so like him.)

He wants to go his own way – that is what we said to each other. He had previously been rather solitary. Now he

seemed to have made friends at school and would cycle to
their houses at weekends, though again he was incommuni-
cative about how he passed the time with them and fended
our questions with a shrug and a monosyllable: 'Play' or
'Ride' or 'Box' (he meant television, not fighting). Mr
Lawrence was rather surprised, indeed he had observed that
Jolyon was perhaps even *further* distant from his fellow
pupils: 'We should not be *alarmed* that he is not one of the
flock, rather the contrary ... ' He was doing as well as ever in
class, and his prowess at rugger was still marked: 'By all
accounts he had a splendid game against Hazelgrove last
week. I suppose your niece told you ... she seems, inciden-
tally, to have made a strong impression on our Mr Bealing.'
Anxious lest I should embarrass him by revealing that he had
been misled – I had no niece, but he had the families of
more than a hundred boys to memorise – I said nothing; I
did not relish the idea of one of his sedulously self-humbling
apologies. I walked from the school back to work, stopping at
the S.P.C.K. shop to confirm that the set of encyclopaedia I
had ordered for Jolyon's Christmas present would be
delivered well on time. It turned out to be a present towards
which he barely bothered to dissemble his indifference; I had
imagined us side by side at the dining-room table turning its
pages. I had imagined him gasping excitedly at its 'exploded'
drawings of liners and aircraft. Instead he leafed through it
impatiently, finding faults; he never opened some volumes.
We hardly saw him in fact throughout the entire holidays,
his last holidays. He insisted on going out on even the coldest
days; it had snowed on New Year's Day and there wasn't a
thaw for three weeks. But he didn't go tobogganing. The
sturdy little sledge you built him stayed in the shed. It's still
there, I dusted it just the other day.

He spent one weekend of the holidays staying at Jonathan's
and so when he said that he had been invited there again for
the weekend of Jonathan's birthday (March 28) we had no
objection. He seemed willing enough to agree to go to
Evensong when he got home. I bought Jonathan a useful
little handbook on the identification of birds, wrapped it in

paper saved from Christmas and gave it to Jolyon to give to him – I suggested that breakfast time on Sunday would be appropriate. Saturday March 27 was a chill, bright day and I watched Jolyon cycle away up the hill with his saddle-bag bulging and his faded red knapsack strapped across his shoulders – he's off on the high road to adventure, I thought. I pottered around the garden in the morning while you went to collect the shoes you were having mended and to have a word with Budden's about the quality of the anthracite. In the afternoon we walked up to Groveley Woods coming back by way of Ditchampton. It was almost dark by the time we arrived home, and very cold indeed. I scolded you for having kept me out so long. We ate shepherd's pie for supper then settled down, you to read and me to knit your Argyle cardigan. We listened to a programme of work by Sibelius on the wireless. At about half past nine I went to put on the kettle and remembered that I had not drawn the curtains in Jolyon's room. So I ran up stairs and did so. I picked up a couple of exercise books that he had left on the window sill, opened his desk to put them away and saw sitting between a bottle of green Quink and one of purple Stephen's the tidily wrapped book that Jolyon had evidently forgotten to take to Jonathan. 'I'll pop down to the corner and telephone his mother,' I said, 'otherwise Jolyon'll be awfully embarrassed. I'll tell them that he'll give it to Jonathan at school on Monday.' You looked at your watch. I fetched some pennies from the jar in the kitchen, put on my coat and walked out of the house. It took a while for someone to come to the phone. 'Oh, Mrs Meades I hope you won't mind my ringing but Jolyon went off this morning without remembering to take Jonathan's present … ' I can't tell, I can't describe the way I felt. I stood there listening with my mouth agape, sick to the pit of my soul. Two girls stood outside the phone box whose light lit their stupid grins. It wasn't Jonathan's birthday, she said, she hadn't seen Jolyon for months. I found myself asking this woman I had hardly met: 'Where is he? Where is he?' The girls giggled. 'I shall ask Jonathan if he has any idea, he won't be asleep yet.' I thought she was never going to come back to the telephone. One of the girls opened the kiosk door and asked, 'You gonner be all night Missis?' 'Damn you,' I said and held the door fast. 'Mrs Good, I don't know what's going on — Jonathan and Jolyon appear to have some sort of pact. But I told him you were frantic ... ' Tilworth, a couple called Welch — 'the property man', something about seeing them in a toyshop. I thanked her, and the girls made animal noises as I stepped from the kiosk.

We walked through the town where the only sound was the rush of voices from public houses. We left the last light behind us. We climbed. Our eyes began to differentiate a hundred different blacks. The cold overcame the heat made by our movement. I shivered as I walked. I linked my hand in yours in your pocket. Small animals crackled undergrowth. A limb of milky mist hung beneath us. The river seemed to boil. I don't know how long it took us. There were lights on all over the house, they poured out into the mist. He was an ape. That man who came to the door was an ape. He shocked me by his size. His voice was that of a creature in a cage. His language was profane. When I saw Jolyon the apeman attempted to strike me. And the women who followed me up the stairs tried to seize my coat; one of them clung to the hem for a moment. The house was a maze. I ran down corridors calling him, saying his name over and over, opening each door I came to, stumbling on rugs. Then I saw another staircase, narrow and steep, and ascended it. I could hear shouts from below me in the house ... The room was like a beacon. There were windows on every side. Jolyon stood with his arms round her neck. She was kneeling and she turned her head to face me. She was pitiful — painted and pathetic and hopeless. She was crying. All around them were toys. Toys of every size and colour and kind, toys that made you wonder at our capacity for useless ingenuity — whoever could need such things? She saw my gaze and sobbed: 'They're such beautiful toys.' I held open my arms towards him, stepped towards him. 'No, Mummy, no.' And he backed away against a great casement window. He looked at me with such hatred; my beautiful boy was bad. 'Go away. I

shan't come. I shan't.' She said: 'You must go home Jolly.
Go on. Go with your mother now.' He winced disbelievingly
and shook his head, 'No, Pammy.' She tried to smile: 'Be a
brave soldier now, darling. It's time you were off.' And he
looked at her just as he had at me. Then he opened the
window.

Alick Welch wrote offering them the sum of £2,000. When
he received no reply he wrote again, offering £5,000. He
heard nothing. The grounds of Tilworth were sold as building plots in 1963-4; the house has been divided into flats. On
October 25, 1971, the Westland helicopter that Alick Welch
was flying crashed immediately after take-off from the
grounds of his house at Frant in East Sussex; he had been
suffering angina.

I'M FINE. DON'T FRET. THIS IS ALL RIGHT. THIS IS
JOLLY GOOD.

Oh So Bent

Danny Garcia was born on February 29, 1940. As a child he was so familiar with the stuff of fairy-tale and romance, and so used to smutty chatter about royal mores that he believed when his mother called him 'My Prince' or 'My dainty Prince' she was hinting at what would one day be revealed to him. Namely: he was a royal bastard and she – this homely coarse soul – was not the woman who had carried him but an imposter charged with his care by a fugitive princess or a hapless beauty tumbled by a king's son. This was a wrong idea. And it filled him with expectations that could never be met. He is still alive and lives in the south of England. He makes arch jokes about his age, dividing it by four and saying things like: 'But how *could* I understand such things, I'm only ten you know.'

Holland Hughes was murdered in 1960 when he was fifty-two years old. His unnatural death matched his beginning, and the position he lay in after the fatal blow indicated his return to the state of uterine bliss he had been ripped from by a surgeon who rhymed as he incised: 'I've tried all I know to ease her. Her child will have to be a Caesar.'

One night, on the eve of one of Danny's birthdays Holland

followed him through the mazy lanes of a Moroccan city. The place was black and strange. Holland wanted to turn back. Danny was drunk, petulant and in lewd voice; Holland hated him in such moments for his sense of adventure and mild curiosity but had no choice other than to stay with him for he could not bear the idea of being alone and unprotected close to the boy hustlers and importunate vagrants and grinning roughs (the folds of their clothes harboured ticks and daggers) who frequented these alleys. Every shadow was that of his murderer, and every hoarse breath too, and every foot that padded along behind him. So he stuck by Danny as a blindman would his dog, despite its errant ways. Danny strutted grossly. His hams were jammed into tight white strides and he looked to all the world as though he was porkily hawking his brawn. He wore an air of happy brutality. Holland was transfixed by the lubric swagger of the bastard's hips, by his promiscuously displayed smile, by his huge smooth hands: 'He used to say they were like bunches of Fyffes.' They reached a crowded square. It was animated and loud. Microtonic music from countless radios mixed in the air. Holland warmed to the sight of people; he was convinced there was safety in numbers, even in numbers so unprepossessing as those here. A man squatted on a Disney patterned rug and pushed a string into his anus and by a corrupted yogic trick made it go against the current of his alimentary canal all through his colons, duodenum and so on and have it exit from his nose. Danny threw him a coin. Holland tushed, he really was in quite a pet. Contempt for a third party is the finger that will always stop the breached dyke of friendship. The truth of that sapphic maxim is shown thus: Against the clitoris-pink cliffs of cloud stood Carrie Mungo. The expiring sun glowed behind her head. She was surrounded by a group of men none of whom was as tall as her – three-inch mules with pompons raised her above them. She had the air of the Madonna in a blasphemously parodic *sacra conversazione* and the mariolatrous apes – all elbows and halitosis – fought for top spot in the impromptu hagiarchy. Danny and Holland gaped incredulously then giggled and

sneered at the sad garrulous woman. Holland had formed a
bitchy intimacy with her in their hotel bar, she was his sort.
She was barren, agalactous, twice widowed and had claimed
Danny with uncritical pride, seeking assurance from him
that his life as an artist was not as fraught as those depicted in
Sherpas of Parnassus. Danny trilled and turned towards
Holland, the very picture of dental health. He grasped
Holland's forearm and stroked it; it was pale as a kelt, and
looseskinned to the touch.

'Ooh, the *doxy*,' one of them may have said to the other
who was thinking just that. Carrie Mungo was eagerly
mistaking the lust of the very poor for gelt and glitter for the
lust of all Moorish manhood for northern (i.e., her) flesh.
She grasped a clutchbag far too small for the banknotes she
had tried to stuff into it. Some of them floated to the ground;
hence the scrabbling of those around her. She had won this
money, publicly, betting at a booth on which of six num-
bered holes a rat would run through when released from a
wire cage by a dwarf with the pocked resentful features of
J.-P. Sartre. He stood there now, across the square, staring at
a dun can he held. It bore the legend 'The Last Supper. (U.S.
Aid Programme)'. It was rat poison and he wasn't sure
whether to administer it to the rat which had disobligingly
scampered into whichever hole Carrie had backed or
whether he should dose himself – he felt that bad about
losing heavily. As they walked past him, arm in arm,
Holland gave Danny a couple of notes and Danny handed
them to him. 'They'll put it on your headstone,' said Danny,
'Easily parted from his wonga.' Then he bent his head
towards Holland's and sang with perfect pitch into the old
steamer's ear: 'Of all the queens I ever knew, I'd choose you
to rule me, my Ro-ose-maree ... Come on, let's hurry back
and I'll gobble up Xenophon.'

'Well,' – here's Carrie Mungo, early the next evening,
addressing Holland – 'watson 'oliday without a flutter?' She
called a roll of long-dead racehorses (Ampersand, Beverly's

Boy, Chum's Son, Corker, etc.) each of which had done it for her. As eager for drama and lots of life as anyone with less than six months to live she entreated Holland to tease her, titillate her with gossip, join in guessing games. Tippling prodigally she clung to the bar and rearranged her tubby buttocks; they were capri-clad and blue veined. Then she assumed the celebrity panellist's vapid air of concentration and shrieked inquisitorially another list of objects that she thought he might have bought Danny as a birthday present: Tray? Table? Lump of sculpture? Big brass paperweight? Leather something or other? Those nice tiles? Holland was playfully, tiresomely secretive and wagged a finger as at a puppy or child: 'I'll make sure he brings it down to dinner.' He adjusted his rakishly tied neck-kerchief, looking into the mirror across the bar. 'I think we ought to go somewhere a bit more *vif* afterwards. Somewhere with a younger feel.'

'Somewhere, you mean,' she prodded him, 'that's got your Amer Picon.' (That nasty gentian liquor was unavailable at the hotel because, so the bow-tie behind the bar had claimed, the delivery drivers were demanding danger money following a recent series of earth tremors. Likely story.)

'That would be just the ticket wouldn't it,' said Holland. He vaulted from his stool. They made their echoic adieus, à tout à l'heure and toodle-oo. Holland sauntered away to the reception desk and asked for the parcel that he had left there an hour or so earlier. 'Meester Ox? Yeh.' The clerk heaved on to the counter a box, nine-inch cube, flashily gift-wrapped. 'Heavy. No? Ooh, ay ay ay.' He shook his hands with pantomimic extravagance, looking for a tip commensurate with the object's weight. Holland obliged, then put the parcel under his arm, keeling ever so slightly left in compensation. He took the lift up to their third floor suite – two rooms, interconnecting bathroom, sea view balconies. He admired, as he was certain Danny would, his choice of wrapping paper and of the gift within it. With a sort of labial anticipation he imagined Danny's thank-you kiss; the firm squeeze of his hand on his shoulder would electrically transmit doting. He wanted it to be dead right, just so. He

97

savoured it so much he wanted to put it off awhile. So he put down the package on his dressing table next to a bottle of Greygone, looked at the bottom of his shoes in case he had stepped in some shit – he hadn't – and flopped on to the bed. He yawned and wriggled on the counterpane, and tried to picture Danny's big open smile. Then he dozed fitfully and all sorts of bright mnemonic scraps presented themselves to him: Clinker overlaps, carvel is flush. Blaise is the patron saint of fellatio, Giles of cripples. Dyce painted Pegwell Bay, Desdemesnes-Hugon painted Camber Sands. The Artotyrites celebrated the Eucharist with cheese. Gesualdo murdered his wife. The Empress Eugénie is buried near a railway line in Surrey. Sado the Wolf and Masoch the Lemming are characters for advanced children. William Whitely was the victim of an alleged patricide. A noise made him start. He sat up, blinked, the room was darker. The sky had darkened, dusk was near, a big inky nimbus covered the sun. There was that noise again, it came from Danny's room. Danny was evidently listening to a broadcast of a progressive jazz combo's concert which was now and again interrupted by an audience's clapping, loud at virtuous solos, hesitantly when it wasn't sure if a number had actually finished. Holland rang room service and asked that a bottle of Bollinger be sent up straightaway; as an afterthought he instructed that it be delivered to Danny's room. He congratulated himself on his prowess as host and provider, mindful of his own dislike of sparkling wine and of the taste that Danny, who drank for giggly oblivion, had for an Australian product called 'Cool Springs Fizzy'. He dabbed his wrists with Pine, dabbed at his hair with brisk fingers, adjusted his collar's roll, drank a slug of Suze from his bedside bottle. Thus prepared he picked up the package and with smug smile opened the door into the interconnecting bathroom. The clapping grew very loud, the concert had evidently ended – he'd always had a fine sense of timing – he swung wide the door into the adjoining room.

And this is what he saw. He saw a small brown boy whose bloodless knuckles were tight around the bedframe and whose head was buried in the rucked folds of bedclothes. He saw a jar of petroleum jelly as opaque as pork lard, a bolster's distended end, a shadow cast in the form of a dromedary, fingers tickling a bald oxter, the albino arch of a foot. Most of all he saw Danny, his birthday boy in manhood's first flush, bouncing high in sodomitical abandon, filling the room with noise, murmuring too: 'Oh quel cul tu as — the real black hole.' And Holland stood there in frozen stride, prey to the truism that afflicts witnesses of the abominable, *viz.*: That such scenes refute the notion of time's obliging adherence to clock-law. Everything conspired to make sure that Holland would remember the details of that room for the rest of his life.

'Tu vas prendre ton pied ou non,' asked the brown boy of Danny, turning his head.

'Hooray. Hooray,' crowed Holland, cuckoldly defiant.

'S'il vous plaît, M'sieur, vous avez une cigarette?' The boy, a sinewy wretch, disjoined himself from Danny. He stared insolently. He was Danny's present to himself, sort of — that was Danny's excuse.

Holland kicked shut the door behind him: 'Get him out of here.'

Danny shrugged. 'Fiche le camp,' he said and jabbed the boy's spine with his foot.

'Je croyais que t'avais pas fini — mais si le M'sieur le veut.' Holland hooked the boy's shirt on his toe and pushed it towards him. 'Ah, M'sieur, vous derangez pas.' He stepped off the bed, bent to pick up the shirt and showed Holland his red anus.

'Dépêchez-vous.' Holland's French was Churchillian. 'Tell this urchin to make himself scarce ... Or I'll put him through the window.'

Like a naughty pet, the boy caught the tone in Holland's voice and hurried to pull on his trousers over his feathery, wintry-thin bush; they were huge hand-me-downs, peg-topped and supported round his ribcage with a perished

99

elastic belt. They were signal evidence of his indigence. Then he knelt on the bed, rummaging for his shoes, jacket and plaid scarf. All sheets tell stories and these (a relief model of a lofty range of peaks with passes and plateaux formed by the giants who once gambolled there), would have proved legible if you knew the lingo. Could you have read there that the boy would refuse to go?

'Quand tu me paies,' he said smirking, arms buried to the elbows in his pockets. Danny, detumescent and edgy, had opened the door in expectation of his exit. A fly entered and made straight for the boy's creamy pomaded mop of curls.

'Va-t'en. Comprends? Uh?' But Danny had neither the props nor the natural advantages of those who habitually utter threats when naked: you need dark skin, fearsome paint, weapons, preparatory intoxication and dancing. The boy knew this, he stared at Danny pityingly and said, matter of fact:

'Tu fais gaffe mec. T'a surement pas oublié mes frères, tous les copains, toute la bande. Il faut faire attention, hein?' And he drew his right index across his throat; the gesture had a terrible literality. It was evocative of a rent vein, a plume of blood, an aborted scream. None of the gang of torpid thugs and guttersnipes among whom Danny had first espied this pretty master looked as though he was a stranger to the quiet blade. Indeed, the pre-foreplay communion had been enhanced so far as Danny was concerned by the boy's base pride in his eldest brother's violent feats. Danny gave the boy the meagre contents of his wallet. The boy laughed:

'C'est incroyable.' He turned to Holland, 'Il est dingue.'

'Je n'ai plus de fric. Je te jure. Ça suffit sûrement?' Danny looked pathetic, pink, quivering.

'Demande à M'sieur,' suggested the boy with aplomb.

'Hol ...'

'Deaf ears, sugar. You should have thought of such things before you let this ... child entertain you.'

'Very well.' Keeping his eyes fixed on Holland he slid from his southpaw the only article of jewellery or clothing that he wore, a gold watch on a gold bracelet. He held it out to the boy. Danny remembers the way the boy took it from him, he pinched the ball of Danny's thumb. Holland, still clutching this year's present, shook his head disbelievingly.

'Danny, how can you? Oh, you bastard.'

The boy scrutinised it as an ogre baron would the offerings of a cowering serf. He put it to his ear, shook it, shook his head, let it drop from his hand to the floor: 'Ça vaut rien. C'est moche – Hong Kong.' (He was wrong about that.) 'Je vais chercher mes frères.' And he went.

The door closed quietly and the room closed in on Holland and Danny.

The walls, the angles where the uniform colour darkened, the ceiling, that encroaching ceiling crazed by webs and deltas oppressed them. It was all so dim. First detail, then outline was lost in the thickening gloom and the shapes they knew became unfamiliar. Then the name Donally filled Danny's head and filled him with fear. Holland clung to Danny like a monkey to a trunk. He whispered that name. It was the name of the defendant in a celebrated trial of those years. Donally the Oedipal Murderer of Wexford. Fergus? Declan? Patrick? Patrick. An oddboy. A backward boy. He had to wait till he was eighteen years old to witness a repeat of the primal scene that had engendered him. With a sure instinct he knew he must rescue his grunting mother. Timing, that was the thing. Now might I do it Pat, he told himself and crushed his father's head with a brick. A brick in the bedroom? Yes.

And just as 'choffoul' (Sheffield) came to be adopted by the Tlonpyg islanders as an expression of high approbation because they prized the flesh-cutting qualities of blades thus marked (Ann Arbor, 'Journal of the Institute of Anthropophagic Studies,' Vol XVIII, No. 3, Summer 1966), so had Holland and Danny, in their island world of two, made Donally the eponym of preposterous half-wittedness. It was their word, but something in the way Holland said it – a systole between syllables and a gasp after – was unfamiliar and horribly understandable to Danny.

Holland, if you like, *corrupted* their private language. He addressed Danny the way that poor boy Patrick Donally had addressed his father the second before he struck him. It was a threat not a joke. Danny felt threatened. He *thinks* he heard an echo of Donally that went: En flagrant délit ... dans mon lit ... dans mon lit. He is sure that Holland backed away from him, looking at him all the while with awestruck repugnance. Holland must often have looked at him that way while he slept, murmuring, nuzzling the pillow: 'You're a milky smooth bit of rough. My pirate. Turk of the Spanish Main.' He wouldn't do that again.

He told Danny to dress. His clothes were scattered about the room. Danny didn't dress. He gyrated his odalisque's hips, stroked his thighs, cradled his scrotum, masturbated. 'Flashing white sergeant — that's what I am,' Danny cackled with authorial delight. His thumb and finger ringed his swollen glans. 'You, Holland, you're so *respectably* bent. You're a net curtains queer, aren't you? No taste for back-gammon have you?' (This was true. Holland's only experience of being buggered had been an unhappy one. Evisceration couldn't have been worse.) 'It takes a clever dick to make an arse smart. How d'you like that?'

'You are making me very very angry Danny. Put your clothes on.'

'You never had a woman either, did you?' Danny railed, careless of the preterite. 'That's another grunt and groan isn't it dear — the beast with two cracks? *Fish*. Ah well ... ' He bent to pick up his polo-neck, laughing. It was tight, a bit damp from sweat and his white hands emerged doing a tyro's tick-tack. It was a struggle to get his head through the garment, he was thus blindfolded when he heard the rush of Holland's breath and the beat of his tread on the floor and felt the blow to his balls. Holland kicked him. For a small man it was a big blow, but then we've all seen the mighty boots of flyweight outside-halves. Danny rolled about, doubled up. He rocked back and forth gasping through the wool. This was the big hurt.

'Why do you do it?' asked Holland. 'You do it, don't you, to break my heart. I gave you a chance and you have to do

102

this. Repayment, that's what it is. Isn't it? I drag you from the mire and this is how you repay me.' Part of that was right. There *had* been a regrettable incident one warm Sussex night. And yes, Holland had been a splendid character witness; he had splendidly repudiated the smears, the tissue of falsehood and innuendo — Danny's words — of that bastard from the Cottage Patrol. Yes, Holland was just about right. Danny was not good at being beholden to people.

Holland sat down on the edge of the bed. He looked most dolorous. He looked older than Danny had ever seen him, as old as the continents and the trees, crumpled. He stared with fixed incuriosity at the spot on the wall where Danny had the day before squashed a fly with a copy of *Photo Apollo*. Today Danny was still writhing on the floor. I suppose that by this time he had got his head free of the pullover. Then at last he stood up and gingerly trekked about the room putting on his other clothes. During this time there was silence. Then Holland said:

'It's easy to betray trust, the easiest thing in the world. Ha. You're all poses really, aren't you Dan. And I'm, well — a sitting duck. I'm obligingly blind. Don't you find?' He sighed as if repining at his credulity, at a life spent playing the boulevardier's dupe.

'Holland — he meant what he said. He has got all these brothers. They'll — God knows what they'll do to me.'

'You are incredible Danny. D'you know that? You are the most unutterably selfish person.'

'I'm serious.'

'Oh, I know you are.' He rather fastidiously crossed his legs. 'Yes, you really are. You Bognor bugger.'

That was Holland's last jest, his final jibe. Danny picked up his birthday present from the chest of drawers where Holland had placed it and threw it at Holland. Now, he threw it underarm and without much force and — if we are to continue to go by his version (there is no other) — without any exclamation more belligerent than 'Pshaw'. Holland's reaction was torpid. He ducked slightly, and too late — but a

thousandth, say, of a second too late. Of course it was a fluke
that the blow to his left temple should have so severely
lacerated the cerebral tissue and cortical veins that he
suffered a subdural haemorrhage. That killed him. Instantly
no doubt and with no sound, moreover, other than that of his
body striking the floor where it assumed the position referred
to before. Danny didn't realise immediately that he was
dead. You don't. It took Danny some time to twig what had
happened. He knelt over the body with patent concern – the
concern, that is, of the nurse rather than of the assassin
making sure his quarry is dead (though the actions of the one
may be indistinguishable from those of the other). He went
on a wild goose chase for heartbeat and pulse. He held a
lather-stippled mirror to Holland's mouth. No luck
– breath's watermark was infuriatingly absent. Danny
thought that it was so *silly* that, as the agent of this momen-
tous physical and chemical change, he was unable to reverse
the process. Not fair. He began to cry. Holland might be an
ocean away, he had gone on holiday for ever.

He knelt between Holland and the death weapon and regret-
ted they had ended on such bad terms. He tried to figure why
he had thrown his only birthday present at his only friend and
had murdered him – murder, murther; it sounded foul chok-
ing obscene, even in repetition designed to rid it of meaning.
He extended a hand like a healer's and laid it on Holland's
heart, warm of course and still. He marvelled that such a
persistent motor which had beaten almost two thousand
million times, through two world wars (first: child, second:
firewarden) and four eclipses could be so easily silenced and
he took a sort of pride in the knowledge that he alone had
found the means to stop it. But that knowledge was nothing
beside his ignorance (which he reckoned would be perpetual)
of Holland's present state, of the metamorphosis that had
occurred unseen within him. Danny switched on the lights
and found himself standing with his head cocked as if to
discern a message in the air. He hoped Holland was climbing
a reincarnatory ladder; but he might not have been. He
might have just become a fly, or every leaf that Danny would

ever tread on, or he might have turned into nothing at all.

When there was a thump on the window pane that made it rattle in its frame Danny extinguished the lights and peered out at the balcony. There was no one there; he was thankful for that – they could climb, these street arabs. And there wasn't a stone or a k.o.'d bird or a pine cone. Nothing. He wasn't surprised. It seemed that the whole world might, with a capricious twinkle, be about to err from all norms. This is the sort of consolatory solipsism that murderers indulge in. He is convinced to this day that he had not suffered an aural hallucination. He stepped out on to the balcony and noticed by the light from the room above that its precast floor was bisected by a crack like a fault in the earth's crust. Birds circled repeatedly and screeched. On the beach the evening sea boomed. The bosky garden beneath him seemed deserted but its big shrubs shaped like arthritic hands surely concealed men who might, with a flourish, a swish of fronds and a leopard's leap, arrest your stroll. Somewhere there against the blackening backdrop the boy and his brothers were shaving their nails with sharp switch-blades. Danny shivered in the warm air, hurried inside.

He thought of Holland in a different way. He thought of him as an inculpatory bundle of dead man's flesh, disposable only with risk. Holland looked like a murder victim; one of his hands was twisted in a way that no sleeper could bear. 'Islam decapitated according to the Koran.' That sentence chilled him, put terror in his heart. (In this context the heart is errant, ubiquitous; it is in every muscle and nerve.) Danny looked about for a cigarette. He found a flattened pack of Casa Sport in the dead man's trouser pocket and lit one; he also found there a wallet whose contents he inspected as though the victim had been unknown to him. He took the money. He could, he realised, lift Holland easily enough; he had been a small man, six inches shorter than Danny and less than nine stones heavy. His toes for instance were no bigger than most men's thumbs. They were dainty in death, encased in neat loafers and pale socks like bandages. Danny, who now weighs almost twenty stones, believes he always despised small men. He certainly despised Holland for having died so readily. Time passed slowly, as for a long-term lag.

There was a knock on the door.

This is when things start to bend a bit, when the rules get broken. Danny swears that he knew who was at the door and that he took that knowledge for granted. There is, he says, no question of his having asked himself how he came by that knowledge. It was as if he had been expecting someone. (He hadn't.) He opened the door to the man from room service. The man had shrunk by about half a foot. He was half a foot shorter than in Danny's (one uses the word with a helpless shrug) *recollection* of him. Danny had never seen him before. Tricky, no? It doesn't get easier. Danny rather tetchily rebuked the man for *having taken so long*; he tapped his wrist. The man made a carious, fawning smile. Then he made to enter the room, but Danny wasn't having any of that. No. He pushed an ample tip into the man's hand, took from him the tray with its ice bucket and glasses, and closed the door. Within a few seconds he was back in the corridor. He found himself yelling at the room servant who now slouched beside the lift door. He found himself waving the bottle, prodding the label and complaining: 'This isn't Bollinger. This is Heidsieck. Where's the Bollinger?' He went into school French. Then the hand of the lift indicator spun wildly. Then an internal echo ripped through his brain, a terribly thirsty gatecrasher demanding Bollinger, Bollinger. Every chamber filled with the name.

'No more Bollinger please sir. No because oh, les livraisons … you understan'?'

Danny flung wide his arms, exasperatedly, and went back to the room. As he stepped into it from the corridor he turned to cast a final spiteful glance at the abject skiv. He was no longer there. Standing where he had been was a giant whose nostril hairs grew long and were waxed to form moustaches auxiliary to those that lined his lips. He was shaving his nails with a dainty knife. His appearance was fantastical, bristling,

106

that of a man who has conjured his own being. This was one that might get different, breathe fire, walk through walls.

Danny thumped shut the door behind him. His face was all puckered with the grin of a lover bringing a ring. He twirled the bottle, all aglow. He cooed: 'Danny!'

Then, of course, he screamed and the bottle tumbled to the floor and the wine hissed over jagged green glass and the ice bucket, shunted by his dervish calf, tipped its load under his feet and more glass fractured. Motes jumped into his eyes. Countless amperes bucked through him. His neck jerked in an abominably taut convulsion as if to snap head from spine. He fell to the floor which was a belligerent place. Like a woman in the avalanche of orgasm he ground his limbs on the scorching emery carpet. Coals fizzed in his mouth. Cherry foam trailed across his face. Then the bolts abated and his distended tongue lolled on his shoulder.

When as a child he used to wonder what being grown up would be like he never conceived of the lack of elation it would all entail, the perpetual anxiety and equivocation, the flight of simplicity. How awful that all he had to look forward to was that room, and the creased bed, and that body that just went on lying there, and these posthumous taunts that came in all sorts of form. For instance: A fart jumped from his anus (once perforated, now perfect – just ask round). Nothing rare about that. But the copious malodour corresponded to nothing that he had eaten or drunk for days – whitefish, mutton, mint tea, white wine, almond cakes and mahjoum could not possibly have combined to make what was the olfactory, anal analogue of international cuisine. That is, steaks and garnish, chicken and garnish, pineapple chunks with everything, glacé cherry everywhere – the kind of food Holland picked at every day of his life.

Danny lay there panting. He longed for happy blackness. Twenty years to the day and he had expelled the waste gases of the man he had killed (*so he says*), had spoken his own name in the voice of the man he had killed, the father he had killed. Holland had been a sort of father to him, he was to become a sort of talismanic meal for him. Danny has no idea what it was that made him scurry on all fours, furtive as a child succoured by beasts, grapple with the fly and french-bearer of Holland's trouser, expose his left thigh and sink his teeth into it. The flesh gave like latex, tasted like pastry. We all know that Aztecs and Apaches ate bits of those they had slaughtered in order to allay their spirits, protect themselves from hauntings. Note Danny's patronym. Garcia. Note too that those Spaniards who are not partially Arab are often of a Mexican mien. Put it this way: maybe his appearance (blond, can o'tan complexion, bulky musculature, fat) belies him. Maybe he was contaminated by the racial memory of the feed consumed by his ancestor Qzctl amidst bloody cacti one sunny day in 1524. This does not obviate his conviction that he was the first man to have eaten the flesh of his own kind; when we make love for the first time we forget that what distinguished our forebears was, precisely, their procreative prowess and we perform the act with which they were necessarily familiar as if it was unknown to mankind. Each of us makes history with every movement.

In the back bar at the Piers and Crown, in the snug at the Nun and Candle, in the poolroom of the Kiss Me Hardy, where a couple of fresh yobs call him Dannibal, in all the other places where he tells his story no one believes him when he says that ripping at a man's flesh is like giving an elephant a blow job. No one doubts, of course, that he has given an elephant a blow job. Fine hairs got between his teeth and the taste of pastry was, he insists, unmistakable. Of pastry, that is, only partially cooked — floury, dank. See the energy a lion uses to take meat from a bone. Imagine then how much he needed; the unnaturalness of man-eating is compounded if the man is raw. Our teeth no more lend themselves to the task than do our rites. Danny's retrospective horror is, he swears, not so much at the meat's source; it is, rather, gastronomic and hygienic. (Few men understand as well as Danny the extent of Fuseli's dedication which required him to eat raw pork and so dream his nightmare canvases.) Danny does not recommend human meat, long pig, in the state that he ate it. He does however testify to the efficacy of his gesture. At some moment in that dark room Holland's skin burst and Danny's mouth was engorged. He swallowed unavailingly and almost choked before he got it down. It announced its slow progress to him. Christ (who will of course never advertise his return because He knows that His devotees, too long fobbed off with bread and wine, will eat Him) alone knows how long it took to descend through him. He crouched there all absorbed, strands of meat like microscopically-viewed spermatozoa or, contrarily, tiny intra-uterine coils speckling his chin. He looked cute as a Murillo urchin.

The phone in the room rang. Somewhere out there people weren't killing each other, eating each other. Danny, for just an instant, couldn't figure what the noise of the bell was. It foxed him. Then he guessed it must be the boy. It wasn't.

''Smee,' Carrie Mungo, singsong and bevvied. 'You two comin' down for your dindins then?'

Danny thought: She has caught me in the act, bang to rights and *she doesn't know it*, does she.

'Lost your tongue then?' No, no, not his tongue.

'No ... no, sorry.'

'*Dan*. Knew it was you. Well ... what was it then?' This question conspiratorially.

'What was ... ?'

'Ooh − you're a coy one Danny. Your *present*, silly. What was it? He wouldn't tell me, Hol. What did he give you then?'

A weapon, that is what he gave him. Strangler's hanky, axe, dagger, gun? No, just an unknown blunt instrument. Danny's mind froze with ham's palsy. But steady − the bones of a plausible story were there ... shopping with Holland and Carrie three days before ... the inlaid tray in an old swindler's window. A tray.

'A tray.'

'Well! The cunning bugger. I guessed it was that you know. I said to 'im. Ooh ... I'll murder 'im when he comes down.'

'I have murdered him. He won't be coming down.' Did he say that? He did, because:

'Your sense of humour Danny!' This, you see, has always been his problem. No one would ever take him seriously. 'It's just like mine. You're like a son to me Dan.'

The son, thinking of last night's grotesque Virgin, saw himself for a moment as Jesus with a tiara of barbed wire. ('You will remember' – Danny exhorted me – 'to put in all the stuff about the Eucharist and cannibalism that I've given you, won't you. And also of course don't forget that Revelations, Zechariah, Luke, Matthew and John Martin all predicted the second coming would happen during an earthquake. Maybe that's by the by though.')

'You *are* like a son Danny.'

'Don't flatter me so.'

'Silly. I've got something for you. And if you don't come down in a moment I'm going to bring it up. Fancy hiding away on your birthday!'

'No. Don't bring it up. Holland's not feeling too good.' There was a meat fibre between his incisors.

'I didn't think he was. He looked like a ghost.'

When was that? The body was still there but the last thing that Danny was prepared to discount was the possibility that hundreds of Hollands, peripatetic former beings, were gliding all over the hotel, all over the earth's surface button-holing people, telling them what Danny had done.

'Cold, flu, something like that ... '

'You give 'im a nice aspirin and hot toddy then Dan. You can't be too careful. Cocks and sneezes spread diseases if you'll pardon me French. 'Is dinner'll cheer 'im up.'

'I don't think we'll be able to make it ... '

'Nonsense. Come on, it's my treat. And I got you a lovely prezzie. At least ... look, the ninny I had engrave it got it wrong and put Donny. You don't mind do ... I didn't spot it till just now, t' tell you the truth. Look, you hurry down and I'll give you a special kiss to go with it. All right? Here I tell you what Danny – you can always change your name. See you in a mo', *Donny.*'

110

He could, couldn't he? Change his name, I mean. From birth he'd been bound to his name, it was the one constant. His face, his brain, his memory, his genitalia and all the rest were in perpetual metamorphosis. But name changes are the legit prerogative of the actor and author seeking memorable euphony (so Edna Grout became Cherie Glasse — but to no avail, she works in a canteen now) and of the harassed immigrant seeking sturdy anonymity. Otherwise it's only crims that go in for it. It didn't seem much of a way out, a progress through Darcy, Danby, Bothwell, Johnson; it went with midnight flits and kiting. There was, though, always Holland. Oh there was Holland all right.

Danny had dashed off his signature countless times. (He still does it, but without having the original for comparison it's impossible to judge the accuracy of the forgery.) Holland Hughes; Danny savoured the name, spoke it aloud over and over, heard it as an entirely different set of sounds from before. Holland Hughes, whose vanity had led him to use in his passport a thirty-year-old photograph. Holland Hughes, whose only living relative was his amputee sister Joanie, a Sydney shark casualty living in Mount Norma, Queensland. Holland Hughes, whose accounts, portfolio and property were well known to Danny. Holland Hughes, whose dead flesh caused Danny's gut to revolt and send him scurrying to the lavatory.

When he had finished and the three skunks that had forced themselves from him lay drowned in the lake (a glassy tin-loaf in cross section) he spryly plucked from the holder on the wall three sheets of greyish, coarse paper, each of them marked 'Hotel Saarda, Agadir'. Then, feeling a lot better, he heaved himself to his feet. He was as clean as anyone with a chronically, professionally abused anus can hope to be, so clean that he could confidently have got run over. He was about to get run over, sort of. He adjusted his dress: 'I dress portside, as the tar said to the tart.' Then he stretched towards the chain that hung from the cistern. He smiled to himself, *I*

am Holland Hughes, and actually laughed a little. He pulled
the chain and pulled the hotel down around him.

The cistern sprang from its brackets and kangaroos of water
leaped up and down, hurling themselves at the ceiling which
was on its way to meet the floor; from their mothers' pouches
smaller roos vaulted here and there. Lots of rats, literal real
rats, breezily forsook their wall cavities and took to the air,
free falling and squeaking with delight as the waste of
hundreds of people was hurled at them. Here came a steel
beam sweeping all before it. Here came another, a makeshift
battering ram wielded by a woman whose chest was a red and
black hole. There was a flying bedstead. A thousand giants
grunted while they trampled millions of potato crisps and
some of them breathed the breath of the coprophage. Like
struck stage flats walls went. One wall went and revealed the
boy and his brother somersaulting, a family circus troupe
with knives between their teeth. The boy's trousers were
swollen, his shirt flapped to give him a humpback. One of his
brothers had slow mad eyes and a segment of his head had
been removed to display the way the insides worked, another
brother had the face of the inquisitive half-wit, like the Yale
of the Beauforts. Now the giants began to bellow. Every
object that happily defied gravity had come from somewhere:
that chair had been made by an old man in Switzerland
whose widow was still alive. That chair had a head in it,
lolling and swaying. A man reeled, another mimed
rowing — this one's jacket was marked as if he had lain on a
magpie and crushed it. Holland cartwheeled by, light of limb
as ever, and blinking. A ball became a knee joint, a blindfolded donkey became a bundle of blankets. 'Time up,'
groaned the giants, tossing cabers indoors. Dancing on the
edge of the world Danny held his head and trembled.

When you die, brickbats and bits of broken stone are
hurled at you in mistake for tickertape by your fellow mortals
all turned out to welcome you down. They cannot tell the
difference. Then the blackness ends and all is light, leucous,
neutral. Once more you are the unborn. In Hell you are a
foetus for ever. You are also unable to shed the memory of

112

jokes heard during your life. You are condemned to immutability. Nothing new will happen. Your brain is full of noises, voices, faces, the number of vampire bats killed to make Atahualpa's fur coat. It is so hot you can see the beast holding the pitch-torch to your belly; his head is shaven, he is ruddily scarred, his arms are tattooed with secret signs and unspeakable words of hatred. Pygmies with American accents fire poison arrows into what were your limbs, your own limbs. You float a lot. Everything goes widdershins and you must masticate raw brains, stiff with blood and hair and skull shards. And you must give your name to a man who patently uses an alias — Mort Tod. Mort Tod says: 'Hi, I'm Mort Tod.'

You hear yourself say: 'Holland Hughes.'

Mort Tod says nothing. He has lips that quiver, and between them dance little spittle jewels. Then you see the rest of Mort Tod's head — he has three eyes. The last one situated, very boldly, in the middle of his forehead. He turns away and says: 'Nice the list.' Mort Tod faces you again, his middle eye impassive, the other two cast down. 'Mr Hughes,' he says — he is gripping an offensive weapon near your feet, a tubular bar, 'Mr Hughes, er you're sure nice?' He bobs his head up and down. He wrings his hands. 'Mr Hughes is dead.'

You hear yourself again, you speak with the jocularity of the doomed: 'But aren't we all.' Mort Tod's eyes flicker. 'I know how you must feel. That's no consolation I know … This has been a terrible thing. But believe me, I'm sure he'll have known nothing about it. *Now*, how are we doing?' Then Mort Tod's middle eye blinded Danny and swayed towards him, a collapsing lighthouse. 'Nice,' said Tod to a wimple with moustache and tits, 'you see Mr Garcia here exercises those eyes of his till they're good as new. Keep your top button undone.' He breathed mouthwash all over Danny's face and winked, man to man. Danny knew nothing of earthquakes. Richter might have been a fugitive Nazi or insane chocolate maker for all he cared. The injuries that he received and was treated for at Kenitra U.S.A.F. hospital by, *inter alia*, Major Tod and Corporal Rossing (Danny says, Thanks Guy and to tell you he never told), included a broken leg and severe facial cuts — he has an inch-long scar over his right eye and another all the way across his chin. Still, they were a small price to pay. Mr John Profumo, Minister of State for Foreign Affairs, sent a very generous £10,000 on behalf of the British people. Everyone rallied round Danny.

Carrie Mungo was saved from death by cancer. They were all dead: the dwarf showman, the boy, his brothers. Danny's gift from Holland lay buried with them, just one of thousands of instruments of accidental death. And Holland was but one name on the roll of 15,000 souls whom God had seen fit to sacrifice so that Danny Garcia might go undetected and unpunished by his fellow men. Thanks be to Him.

Danny tells everyone what I've told you. Few of us believe him. The earthquake at Agadir occurred soon after 11 p.m. on February 29, 1960 — not, as Danny has it, at about 8 p.m. There is no record of survivors of the disaster having been transferred to Kenitra. There is no record of a Major Tod serving at that time in the U.S.A.F. Medical Corps. The name of the hotel was Saada not Saarda. And so on.

Rhododendron Gulch

You know the subs. Brillo-pad hair, polychromatic teeth –
gamboge, green and swarf – jackets constellated with vomit
and faecally stained trousers, threadbare coats fastened with
rope, complexions cracked like a teapot's inside – the
increases in the price of which beverage they know very well
even though they tend to forgo it in favour of Lanliq and
Eldorado and Merrydown (what happy names). They aren't
all winos. Some subs were punks once and still sport the
uniform, though bondage trousers tend to hamper the
already gawky movement of glue victims and make them
look more blocked than they are. You know them. Their
habitats are usually in what we have learned to call the inner
city – of whose malaise they are no doubt a product and a
symptom etc., etc. (*Subsistence – Environmental and
Material Correlatives*, D. Oss and A. L. Key, University of
Essex, 1979). Camden, Camberwell, these are the places
you find them, near vents expelling warm caff blasts or
happily deaf to the traffic that whizzes past their glassy plots.
You do not expect to find them in Surrey.

'No you don't often see them. Don't know where they
crawled out of. Come down here for a day out. Awayday.

115

Eh? Ha!' Mike did the high-tar cough that was his laugh. Though his National Service had been all jankers (flattening corrugated iron with a lawn-mower) he knew that this was the answer. Or maybe labour camps were the answer. 'Used to have them, you know. Nothing nasty, mind you. Stopped this, though. Scots mostly.'

He viewed with distaste the efforts (unsuccessful) of a male sub to wrest a bottle from the one female in the group of five who were sullying the green at Esher. Mike was a guard. He preferred to be called Michael but was, truly, one of life's Micks, so I shall call him Mike. *Je pense donc je compromets.* He preferred to be called a security consultant but was, truly, a dog-handler with elementary burglar-alarm nous; his C.V. was thick with bouncer euphemisms. So I shall call him a guard.

Now, his antipathy to subs. No sub would ever employ him, no sub would bother to bust into a place that he had fitted with an alarm. These people present no threat to property but their marked indifference to gainful enterprise is a threat to the idea of ownership, a sort of reproach even. They couldn't be bothered to nick anything worth nicking — which must, to Mike, have seemed wayward. They had no respect for themselves, for their own privacy, for money, for their health, for their lives. And yet for all their lousy clothes and incoherent garrulity they seemed happy, if a gingivitic grin and a salute with a bottle can be taken as signs of happiness. Their deaths no doubt will be inglorious, unnoticed, urban. Their deaths will not be Surrey deaths.

'That,' said Mike, pointing with a thumb over his shoulder as we drove along, 'is where Mike Hawthorn got his.' Now that was more like it — a 3·4 Jag cartwheeling through a winter's afternoon, the suggestion that the golden boy had been dicing on open roads with a friend, the conviction that the bogey that hung over the Ferrari team of that age was again at work: Peter Collins was dead at the Nürburgring and Luigi Musso in the cornfields outside Reims and now Hawthorn himself. 'Great driver,' said Mike, and accelerated. I put on my seat-belt.

116

Here is the house where Len lives. Up there in a fork of an oak that rises above the cliffs of rhododendron is a camera. In the lodge (all of thirty yards from the house) is a screen. Mike arranged for their installation. There has been only one burglary since then. Surrey is in the burglary belt. Some of those who get burgled are burglars themselves, though not perhaps that many. Most greengrocers and 'metal brokers' who do successful jobs (or at least keep the loot) move out to Epping, Ongar, Chingford and so on. That is the blue-collar gangster belt whose pretensions to respectability are thin; the villains who go there like to be on first-name terms with footballers. If what Mike said is anything to go by and if Len's example was anything to go by, Surrey gets a more ambitious sort. The sort who wants to fit in with people who are patently legit – the embezzler, the book-cook, the man who has 'laundered' his money. Cowboys with shooters not welcome.

That's not to say that when Len first moved in among the birches and the bracken he was not a bit rough. Now he can boom 'jumbo gee and tee ice and slice twice' with some aplomb. Then he really didn't know the form. Nigel tells this story: Len and the Mrs Len of those days took to going to the right pub at Saturday lunch-times. They did not throw their money about, did not order particularly fancy drinks and they dressed down, tweedily anyway. A couple of days before Christmas the place was crowded and loud, all backslapping and parcels. A normally well-behaved dog called Dusty found it too much to bear and joined in the jollity, jumping hither and thither, leaving poochy paw marks on coats fashioned from the skin of fellow quadrupeds, causing tables to lurch and drinks to spill. No one minded much save the couple who owned the creature, a cravat and a headscarf who threatened him with expulsion to the car outside (period colour requires a Healey 3000). The dog was disobedient, almost tumbled into the open fire at one point.

Len caught headscarf's eye, she looked embarrassed and exasperated. Dusty did another leap, more circus than shire (a further source of embarrassment) and a Tattersall check shirt muttered something like 'ruddy hound'. The next time

117

that Dusty skidded to a halt by him, melting icicles of slobber dripping on to the floor, Len acted. He punched Dusty on the side of the head. Not a playful cuff but a proper Hackney sandwich. The dog keeled over, very surprised, made an eldritch whimper and lay wriggling like a decapitated eel. The silence was loud as the clash of tweeds in the bar. Len didn't get. He gave Dusty's owners a bonhomous collusive nod and turned back to Mrs Len. Half the people in the place turned out to be vets, the other half canine defence vigilantes. Len had acted in good faith and all he got for his trouble was a drubbing from men who liked to be called Major and some paunchy perpetual prefects.

He retreated to the clubhouse of the golf-course on to which his house backed, where he did not have to pretend to be poor, where Mrs Len could experiment with mixtures of sweet drinks and feed the one-armed bandit, where he could get to know people like himself and — this was the middle Sixties — some of the showbiz people who were moving in and hadn't got stuffy. But he was still careful about who he mixed with, and took a rod at Royalty on the Hampshire Avon where he learned to talk about *killing* salmon although (says Nigel) if no one was around he would fish with a worm.

I do not know who designed Len's house and neither did he. But if names like Imrie and Angell, Oswald P. Milne, P. D. Hepworth, Oliver Hill and Basil Oliver mean anything to you, you'll get the picture. They are the epigoni of Lutyens and Voysey and Prior; they are the men of the Teens, Twenties and Thirties of this century who were responsible for many of the houses on those private estates which are peculiar to the home counties and which achieve their apogee at Wentworth and St George's Hill, though there are dozens of others not much less splendid.

Let's look at Len's. Let's call it Lenden, which by the standard of this estate is rather a modest name (Beech Wynd, High Breath, Bom Clima, Sagittarian Villa, Mei-Tan, Turpin's Forge and, styled with huge humour or lexical incuriosity in black Beggarstaff lettering on a hammered copper background the home of, presumably, Irene and

118

Albert, Renal). Such a conjunction of house and flora is the very stuff of north Surrey, where loam, clay and sands favour the rhododendron, a shrub which will not do well on the chalk and lime of the downs. You approach Lenden up a winding pink road with the fattest sleeping policemen you ever saw, sleeping policemen grown obese from pornographers' backhanders. I suspect that Mike had done a detour to avoid taking me in through the main gate of this estate, for the guard there — ersatz U.S. cop outfit and walkie-talkie — was from a big heavy-duty outfit. Another guard from the same outfit was leaning against his Land-Rover talking to a couple of men who were trimming the copious grass verges. 'They're not real pros,' said Mike, 'merchant bleeding bankers if you ask me.'

There seems to be leafmeal on the verges all the year round, no matter how sedulously they may be swept and raked; they also display an assortment of white posts that support black knobbly chains and lots and lots of staddle-stones, which are assumed to be something to do with ancient mushroom rituals. Every now and again you glimpse green pantiles and white render, or ochre tile-hanging and sculpted thatch, hairdressers' thatch; the balance between ostentation and seclusion is a delicate one. There is a cramped self-consciousness in the way that these houses are designed to be seen whilst keeping up the pretence that they are not intended to be seen.

Lenden sports an impressive set of features — that thatch, eyebrow dormers, not too regular half-timbering and plenty of it, lead lights, massively rustic door furniture, verandas supported by tree trunks, sub-Jekyll garden which — artful touch, this — turns to wilderness at its edges thus kidding the place's occupant (who of course knows otherwise) that it extends infinitely, when on two sides there are houses and on a third the golf-course. The house is built at the top of a steep slope and on one side has three storeys. The kitchen is then on the ground floor although there is a billiard room beneath it. Remember this.

Mike pointed with pride to his burglar alarms, some of

them immediately apparent, others well hidden. 'You need more than one circuit.' While we were wandering round the house, which the more you look at it the more it looks like half a dozen cottages ornés piled upon each other, the current Mrs Len turned up, making the number of cars up to five. She was dressed for riding, made up for work on a make-up counter and had a Husky with lots of suede straps and jetting on it. Mike was evidently a bit wary of her, thought her a bit stuck up and quite liable to do the dirty on Len, one of whose wives shopped him to the Inland Revenue when she received what she considered an unsatisfactory settlement, another of whose wives left him for a Spanish professional basketball player.

While Mike went into the house for 'a meeting' with Len I wandered round the edge of the golf-course. Who are these people who play on weekday afternoons? What is that roar? The Surrey puma? The tigers that Gordon Mills, sometime manager of Tom Jones and Gilbert O'Sullivan, keeps in his back garden? Is that the house where Ribbentrop lived when he was ambassador here? Do these people actually believe that this is the countryside? Or — and this may be closer — are these places London's equivalent of t'top, the bit in all provincial towns where new money goes and where a provincial boy who has made his pile is bound to end up, given that the social topographical map of inner London marks no place like t'top? You can imagine that it would have been Epstein rather than Lennon who thought that Weybridge was a clever place to live; Lennon moved there when the Beatles still wore suits and were showbiz, not youth culture. Tom Jones and O'Sullivan are of course showbiz.

In the car-park of the golf-club are row upon row of brand-new Mercedes, Range Rovers and bogus Range Rovers (Matras? Chevvies?) with heavy-duty tyres. They really do think they're in the country. A couple of men wearing trousers of Taiwan plaid, cashmere roll-necks and hefty sheepskin coats eye me suspiciously. Culpability for undetectable computer crimes rests heavy on their shoulders like Ruritanian epaulettes that I alone can see. Walking back across the sandy hillocks of the links I see one magpie and add it to the others I have seen recently — silver, good. Then I see two Dobermanns — how does the conjugation go? One for panic, two for terror ...

Later Mike told me about an interesting way of incapacitating these beasts. He also pointed out a house where there were kennels in the bedrooms, but no dogs. He was not much interested in whether this was or was not countryside proper. He grew up in a rural slum on the Kent border, one of the shack colonies that called itself the 'London Alps'. Tatsfield now looks like a low-rent version of an expensive private estate — the roads are unmade and the hedges are privet and ragged and the houses are mean; but there is the same striving for flashy privacy and the same huddling up together. What he wants to talk about is the venture that he hopes Len will fund. He has ascertained that the railings torn up from London squares during the war were not melted down to be refashioned as munitions but were dumped secretly (he used this adverb half a dozen times) in the Thames estuary off Sheerness. With his diving know-how and contacts and Len's money behind him they could both *really clean up*. Did I know the prices you could get for these railings? Did I know that they weren't just scrap but *old?* Did I know that architectural antiques was real business with knockers just like the kosher antiques business?

Look, he could show me a house built entirely out of bits of old houses. He could show me a house which a builder had built for himself by gannexing the materials, i.e. stealing them from his own company — this was a dodge that Mike particularly admired, though he was unsure how to execute it himself, I suspect. Did I want to see a house where a friend of his had gone to buy a second-hand stereo, found an orgy in progress (4 p.m.), bought the machine and left half a dozen disgruntled orgiasts complaining to their host that it wasn't the same without music? Yes. It turned out to be a ringer for the one in the Margaret Tempest drawing on the endpapers of Alison Uttley books.

121

Nigel's father was one of many men who have at one time or another been called 'the most passed over major in the army'. He eventually resigned his commission in the mid-Fifties, established a small business manufacturing plastic bottles (which were a novelty then) and died of cancer ten years later. Practically the last thing that he learned before he died was that the van taking wages to his employees had been held up and robbed in a lane near Farnham. The very last thing that he learned before he died was that the robbery had been done by Nigel and two ne'er-do-well brothers, a cashiered squaddie and a fence erector, whom Nigel had fallen in with. The former squaddie was sent down; the fence erector got probation; Nigel got a conditional discharge – remorse, the shame he'd brought on his family, bad company, the fact that he'd been at Stowe, etc., etc. What he learned from this outing was not to get involved with half-wits who do a job, get badered in a pub and tell anyone who'll drive them home that they have done a job. Nigel's mother – a woman of foolish pretensions by all accounts – sold the house (designed for himself by the painter William Desdemesnes-Hugon) and beat a hasty to Bournemouth, dypsomania, second marriage, Barbados.

When I say that her pretensions were foolish I mean that she didn't adhere to Hitler's dictum about the size of lies. She called a house a 'hice' but lived in fear of getting found out; thus she merely elevated her father from being a bank manager to director of a merchant bank. Foolish; she didn't realise that unless you are *very* implausible you will not get found out in Surrey, since everyone is at the same game. You brag about your background or you exaggerate it or you invent it or you really shout about your lack of it.

Back to Nigel. Three years in London being a sort of exquisite, a King's Roadie (knew Brian Jones, can remember the greys from the *NoW* who trailed him in a furniture van, recalls an hallucination where the side of that pantechnicon outside Ashburn Mansions falls away revealing a reporter with bins and a photographer in what they had turned into a rudimentary sitting-room – lots of bottled beer and copies of *Penthouse* and, ugh, Festival of Britain furniture; this was in the days when Ducky Fields had only just discovered Deco, let alone the Fifties. It was then that Nigel cottoned on to antiques in the all-Arab Leighton House eclectic style.

Off to Fez, Back to a conviction for attempting to import kif. Hefty fine — again the boy was basically a good sort, and had to contend with having been at Stowe ... Back to habits born at Stowe and overdeveloped in Moghreb. In the Tangerine sodomite sodality which was still mourning the loss of Joe (and Ken), at a party at Cap Spartel, Nigel met an actor whose name it would be too expensive to reveal. Here's a good name for him: Roger Roger. Nigel fell in love with R.R., had him as a character witness, though God knows how much good that did. Imagine that party at Cap Spartel: hibiscus and bougainvillaea, balmy breezes, strong-arm balmy, an Hispanic bungalow, a fountain. Now through this fountain came champagne (O.K. Cordoniu and Vouvray and Saumur) plus a little electric shock. So when a glass touched the liquid there was a tiny little 'ping' for all the guests to go bananas about. Easy to imagine what happened later, when the guests were badered. They were all men, you know, and they really were badered; and staggering and stooping they dipped what we call their male organs into that fountain. You can imagine the results. R.R.s rogering, roving eyes met Nigel's. Earth moved; earth quaked; did you know that Robin Maugham ground his teeth when he slept? Every night an Agadir.

Their life together — that of Nigel and R.R. was v. cosy. Acting in the popular telly series '—' R.R. made more bread than Hovis. They lived at R.R.'s house in what you might call 'Durbridge' after the place's laureate. R.R. was entirely trusting, so taken with Nigel. So taken with Nigel that Nigel took him for £25,000. Nigel just wrote out cheque after cheque to himself. He was an adept of R.R.'s signature. When a bonehead at the very caring bank realised what was going on, R.R. was informed but Nigel intercepted the letters. At last Nigel was circumvented and R.R. was called in to face the bank manager. R.R. didn't want to press charges but the bank did, it insisted. But Nigel saw a way out, namely Anthony Mahoney, soi-disant Viscount Mullagh. (Mullagh is a place near Quilty, in Clare.) Mahoney was a queen who helped Nigel in his antiques business. He was also prone to the most terrible depressions. Nigel persuaded him to do this. He got him to go to London, sign in at an hotel (that nasty Seifert drum in Knightsbridge), take an O.D., send a letter to Bow Street police station stating that he, Mahoney aka Mullagh, was the sole recipient of the money from the ripped-off cheques and that he was killing himself out of contrition, that Nigel had not benefitted from this fiddle.

Now, by some dreadful fluke this letter reached Bow Street before M. aka M. had made the big jump. Boys in blue, ambulance wallahs, stomach pumps. When he came round M/M. was in a very different mood, told all, landed Nigel in the shit.

This time Nigel was sent down. He quite enjoyed prison, for anal rape was rife; he likens sex to a treasure-hunt: 'You never know what you're going to find — Brasso cans, boxing-gloves, milk bottles. Who knows? We in the great struggle are so inventive.' Inside Nigel met a man who had stolen some Greek icons but instead of reselling them had *leased* them out. This gave Nigel the idea of doing the same with furniture, objects, clocks, etc. The only difference between Nigel and the icon man is that Nigel actually bought the objects he would lease. It may be done elsewhere, I don't know. I do know that Nigel's instinct was dead right and that Surrey was just the place.

'M'dear, they have *no* taste. Not a teeny weeny bit. And what people with lots of dinari and no taste have is *crazes*. One week they fill the place with so many putti that it looks like an orphanage, the next week they read that Milady Gleet has gone chinois or vindaloo flock and have to go there themselves. Plus ça change, plus c'est fric. If they owned the stuff they wouldn't want to change unless they could unload it with yield. They are very keen on *yield*. Wot yield yer get on yer Roller, Tel? My way well ... I'm sure they think I'm muggins. In fact a little birdie tells me so.'

Len and Len's wives have patronised Nigel since he started. Obviously they buy a lot of stuff too and Lenden has rooms that are like museums of long-past fads – busy gilt and green rococo stuff, Sixties spaceship plastic stuff, some nightmarish art nouveau stuff ... Nigel would like to buy some of it but Len paid such silly prices for it that he'll only sell at even sillier prices. Matter of pride, and yield of course. 'But what does he expect. Really. You only have to take one look at him. He is uneducable. You can tell the poor man nothing. He probably thinks ... I don't know – that Chippendale was a potter or something.'

Nigel once thought that Nijinsky was a dancer. In a pub in 1970 he heard the name mentioned and looked round: 'He was really rather farouche. Not your run of the mill balletomane at all. Vest and tattoos and Brylcreem on his sideburns and what some girls call buggers' grips. And a rather rank smell, very very ouvrier. Then some of the great unwashed put on their jungle music so I couldn't hear what my man was saying and I really disliked the look of his chum. Anyway I hung about looking very Dietrich and when he went for a Fraser Nash I followed ... ' Nigel showed me the scar across his jaw. Nijinsky was the racehorse. The man was not a balletomane. The man took exception to Nigel's importunity and hit him so hard that he fell and cracked his jaw on the edge of the urinal. Nigel had to have stitches in the wound and was treated with derision by the publican and ambulance attendants. Even without the scar it is hard to imagine him looking like Dietrich. In fact Nigel looks a bit like a sub who has had a lucky break.

He has a disastrous Nagasaki complexion and the sort of lank blond hair that always looks dirty. Had he been born into a lower class I suppose he might have become a sub. Had he been born a generation or two earlier he would almost certainly have become a remittance man and Denholm Elliott would have played him in the film of this piece. For someone who knows absolutely *nothing* about racing he has a rather racecourse look about him. I don't mean that he wears bookies' checks — do bookies still wear them? Rather that he wears the sort of clothes that young men with bins and trilbies, who seem to know all the owners, wear. Waisted jackets, rather tight-bottomed trousers, heftily striped shirts with high collars of the sort that are eternally associable with *Town* magazine. His taste did not extend to food. While he would laugh at the thought of Len and Suzi (Mrs Len) eating scampi and watching Jack Jones or Mel Toupée at the Country Club he would live off toast and his prowess as a cook was about equal to that of the average motorway caff chef.

Nigel suspects that Len has an interest in the Country Club, a place whose architecture and punters about match its food. It is run by a former crime reporter who suddenly got rich, said goodbye to N.A.A.F.I. stabbings, truncated trunks in trunks, and all the stuff that a proper page three is made of and became an entrepreneur, as they say. Nigel was never sure where Len's money came from till he got friendly with Suzi, who knows where some of Len's money comes from: the sources are actually pretty predictable — property and porn mostly. One of Len's companies produced the first 'adult' jigsaws in Britain. Another produced such films as *Eat me in St Louis, Bulky Chunk, Beaver Fayre*. Another has turned these and others into video tapes. Another owns some cheerless suburban offices. Another has developed some villas near Estepona. And so on. Len ceased some time back to play as active a role as he once did. His idea of an active role was, say, to suggest to a chip-shop owner that he might like to vacate his premises by throwing the shop's cat into the deep frier. 'Without batter,' said Nigel.

After all this I rather wondered if meeting Len was such a good idea. When, after a game of pool on which I had won what Len called 'a carthorse', i.e. a big pony, and after about a third of a bottle of Armagnac I found myself asking Len about deep-fried cat, I thought it was a very bad idea. However he merely seemed rather surprised that I should be interested; he evidently considered it quite unremarkable.

Maybe it is something that all property men do – an everyday ploy like excrement on the doormat or kippers in polythene under the floorboards.

Len was more interested in telling me about how he had shot a swan with a twelve-bore. 'Yes,' I said sympathetically, 'they are a fisherman's bane.' Though I had not quite worked out why anyone would carry a twelve-bore when he was fishing. Len looked at me with disbelief. Len was big and tanned with a wide corrugated neck and a go-getting growth of grey chest hair that was anxious to show itself to the world. His look of disbelief was minatory. 'You're joking. I wanted to eat one. Never again. I got a chill wading in to get the bleeder. I blew its head off and it started floating away.' You can see, can you not, the blood bespattered bundle of white down making its posthumous escape. 'Like rope. It tasted like rope. Rope dipped in sump oil. Not worth it. Didn't warrant the bother. Nothing like duckling. I'm not bothered about food any more ... when in Rome. Look, you eat great stuff in Seville, and we go to this little place up in the hills towards Ronda, but there's no point in looking for that here. If you go out here you stick to smoked salmon and scampi and the avo – that's what they know how to do round here. Regional specialities.'

Would – variation on my one question – he like to live in the country? Once again the minatory stare of disbelief, or maybe incomprehension. 'Look, we got the golf-course at the bottom of the garden. We got so many squirrels it's like a zoo. You come upstairs and I'll show you one of the finest views in England.' He was referring to a great sweep of bosky hillocks, sands and heath rather than to the suede walls and vast hooker-size bed with electric control panels. He picked up a field guide to British birds and opened it proudly; many species had a tick and a date beside them. He thumped a page with a big pumice-scraped forefinger: 'I've seen all those from up here. Know why they come here? Because there's no farmers pulling up the hedges and knocking down the trees and that. No insecticides.' This little burst of unrestructured eco-prop was most surprising, but I suppose that in every

127

hunter there is a zealous conservationist waiting to get out.
And of course he had a point; much of Surrey is at least
illusory countryside, while the 'true' countryside of much of
the rest of England is being sacrificed to the agricultural
industry and being parcelled by quangos into leisure trails
and picnic sites and car-parks with log-cabin lavatories.
Surrey attracts few tourists — children hiking on Box Hill and
interesting young men who 'collect' the houses of Horace
Field and Leonard Stokes and Thackeray Turner. Pukka
tourists go to pukka tourist country like Dorset, where you
can pay to watch cows being milked by hand.

'Osteo-inertia,' Len again, talking about Nigel, 'that's
what they used to call it in the R.A.F. Osteo-inertia — bone
idleness. He's lazy and he thinks everyone else is lazy too.
He's a bit dense is our Nigel. He's got form like this.' Mimes
fisherman exaggerating. 'Did you know he held up one of his
brownhatter's clubs with a shooter and got away with *a bottle
of Scotch*. I know he done it. The filth knows he done it. But
our boy's got a close friend, a bum chum like, who's a stipe.
And they just happen to have been dancing the night away at
the precise time. He'll come to a sticky end, our Nigel. He
isn't clever enough to be too clever by half. That's good, isn't
it.'

Nigel did come to a sticky end and so did Len and so did
Mike. It was all very neat and pretty, like the Surrey
countryside or a house by Lutyens — nothing grandiose or
epic.

Len had still not decided whether or not to finance Mike's
estuarial salvage jag, so Mike took to calling at Lenden on a
variety of pretexts in order (a) to remind Len that he was a
loyal servant and (b) to enlist Suzi's support and have her
petition Len. When Len came back from golf or London,
Mike was about — chatting to Suzi or armed with a catalogue
full of new and better burglar alarms or adjusting the angle of
the camera that overlooked the entrance. Sometimes when
Len came back Suzi was nowhere to be found. Len would

walk round the house with a Double Boswell in his hand cooing uxoriously; then he would try the gaudily painted gypsy caravan in the grounds where Suzi sometimes like to sit with a thick powerful paperback; then he would ring the stables where Suzi kept Justyn, her grey (and where novices could have their equestrian efforts videotaped for 'comment' by a well known eventer). Then he would sit down and pour himself another Double Boswell and watch pro-celebrity golf on the J.V.C. When Suzi came in she would say that she had been riding. Len did not let on that Bonnie at the stables had not seen her.

One hot summer's day Len had to fly to Malaga in order to arrange backhanders for some planning officers. However, the flight was cancelled (Andalusian baggage handlers demanding a living wage) and Len drove home in a most irate frame of mind, sweating copiously and ruing the day that Franco had died, wondering just how he was going to get his new project started. He turned into the drive, got to the house, braked violently and sent a spray of gravel stones bouncing against the side of Mike's car. Indoors he called out 'Suzi', dumped his brief-case on a leased Caroline chest in the hall and marched into the racquets-court-size sitting-room. There at the other end, beside a rumpled Michelin man sofa, was Suzi, stooped and struggling into a pair of trousers. There on the carpet was a pair of Church's chukka boots. The cuff of a striped shirt protruded from beneath the sofa.

Lots and lots of percussionists began a rehearsal in Len's head and hundreds of well-wishers chucked black confetti into his eyes. He pushed Suzi on to the sofa and said: 'Where is the bastard?' He marched into the kitchen, removing the door from its hinges. The top of a ladder was at the window; Mike's face appeared, looking furtive and followed by his naked shoulders and chest. Len roared. Mike seemed surprised. Len, who had the strength of a man half his age and twice his size, picked on a preposterous pedimented cupboard (no shelves, no use) which Nigel had forced on them, pushed it hard (God, it was heavy) so that it toppled and with an *almighty heart-bursting effort* hurled it through the window. Inside the cupboard was Nigel, who was counting the number of times he had just avoided being caught *in flagrante delicto* and was wondering what was going on. It was like being at the fair when you are little, the noise and the dark and the sweeping through space. The cupboard landed on the terrace below with a crisp thud. Mike was beneath it clutching a burglar alarm. Nigel's body somersaulted from the cracked cask and came to rest in the lavender of the herbaceous border. In the kitchen Len's lips turned from purple to blue.

The Brute's Price

The post-mortem examination of Susan Jessica Hand who was going on thirteen years old showed the presence in her vagina of semen, saliva bearing the trace of alcoholic spirit, and sheep's faeces. She had had sex just the one time, just before the end of her life. She was described as having been 'full of life', 'vivacious', 'happy-go-lucky', 'helpful', 'a promising fencer'. These are the attributes invariably granted to such girls. Had she grown up she might have continued with her painting – she was good at that too – she might have married, reproduced herself, left him. Instead she got all the bother in one go, she got it over with early on, quickly. This much is certain: On the evening of Friday May 20, 197– she was alone in the flat above the building society office of which her father was the manager. She ate supper (baked potato with cottage cheese and peanut butter, coleslaw salad, a satsuma) whilst watching television. At about 8.10 her very best friend Frances Rolls telephoned to suggest that they take an earlier bus than usual to Bournemouth the next day. They talked about some boys they had met the last time and Frances could hear the television, 'an offbeat tragicomedy with David Niven and Gina Lollobrigida' most likely. Susan said that she had just painted her nails with her mother's new varnish, a shade called Ravishing Night; the bottle was found, together with a bottle of Cutex, on the floor beside the sofa. It was the only red mark on the carpet. Frances recalls that she admonished Susan for calling Duncan Jamieson 'a thally' and told her it was immature and hurtful, then she laughed and called Johnny Buckingham, the one Susan liked, 'a bif'. Thalidomide, spina bifida – these are the sources. They giggled together. You can bet that Susan put her hand across the lower part of her face.

Michael and Joyce Hand, who would never be grand-parents, stopped on the way back. The Jolly Kindlers has floodlit gardens and trellises bright with bulbs like fruitgums, it looks welcoming. It is not surprising that they blame themselves but, really, the twenty minutes they spent over a large Laphroaig (till then his favourite drink) and a rather daring half of scrumpy made no difference for when they arrived home at 10.40 Susan had been dead for at least an hour. That, anyway, was the opinion of the police doctor whose breath smelled of mints and who kept a stethoscope in his ears so that he might not hear 'what a soviet of armchair pathologists has to say'. There was no blood. There was a cyanotic bloom on her face, her lips were the colour of nearly raw steak, the handmade stains on her throat were marble blue. The ball of knitting wool in her mouth was as green as an apple. The cushion her face was buried in was patterned with birds, leaves, thorns. Yet when Joyce Hand saw her only child prone she was not alarmed. Susan looked so *odd* with her arms tucked beneath her trunk that Joyce thought she must be doing a yogic exercise; she was at the age for crazes. Her pose suggested neither the act of rupture and emission that had occurred nor the force used to smother her. (Maybe the force hadn't been that big. Maybe it hadn't needed to be – after what had happened maybe she had raggedly submitted to the dazzling anaesthetic cushion.) She had certainly fought to begin with. She had – this is speculative, but the police and Kevin Dickon concur – heard a noise downstairs at the back, where a door gives on to a walled, flagged yard, and had gone to investigate. The intruder, it was thought, had not realised that access could not be had to the building society office save through the street door. The rape was thus considered to have been 'compensatory', i.e. of the type specified by Edward J. Ritchie in *Reactive Action: The Potency of Failure* (Annals of the Duane Institute of Criminology, Tulsa, No. XXXIV, 1974). Dr Ritchie's assertion, which carries the mighty weight of a blinding truism, is that rape, forcible entry of a body, is analogous with burglary, and that the individual who undertakes one will very likely undertake the other. Therefore the thwarted expectation and frustration experienced by a burglar who has failed to gain entry may be obviated by sexual assault. Dr Ritchie has nothing to say about murder. Subsequent cases were to indicate a different motivation. There was nothing to link them with attempted burglaries. Unofficial police opinion was that Susan gave a previously non-violent thief 'a taste for young 'uns'.

As she was dragged up the stairs (a sliver of pink shoe leather was found on the third riser from the top) and across the sitting room (the carpet nap showed the trail) she didn't know that the man she screamed at and with whom she pleaded was The Hoody Brute, she never knew that. Mr Bowns who had just left the perilously terraced allotments behind and saw the tail lights of a car in the lane but thought nothing of it didn't know it was The Hoody Brute. Even the Hoody Brute didn't know he was The Hoody Brute — Kevin Dickon had yet to coin that infamous and, very likely, wrong name.

You will see just how Dickon got it wrong, you will see too the consequences of his having got it wrong. You will see that it wasn't really *his* wrong idea to begin with, just one that he had quietly lifted. But I must watch what I say; Dickon has three million readers every day and I have only you. Besides, it was indisputably Dickon that thought of the reward.

'Ssst ... erm – Graham. Yeh?'

'No, don't be soft Ralphy. Don't even *like* Graham. Give us a smokey bacon will yer, there's a luv.' Kim lifts her chin which is the shape of a plump almond, peers ahead of her, paints a dense uneven line beneath her left eye, opens her mouth and crunches the oily sliver of potato that Ralphy stokes into it. 'Nice ... C'mon, try again. Name the Name,' she cries, jaunty and bossy. 'Less 'ave 'nother crisp.'

'You got me 'ere, erm ... ' Ralphy swigs from his tin of beer, 'lesh see. Ah! Shtephen?'

'Yer ... !' Kim gets up as quickly as her pregnant belly will allow. She gets up so quickly that the formica-top table goes over and so does the tin of blusher, mascara, lipgloss, etc., and the party pack of crisps and the box of Dairy Box and the photographs of Sean and Trudy in their lizard-skin frames and the three Christmas cards and the Lovewear International catalogue and the bronze vase of paper flowers and the Corona bottle. They all clatter to the floor while Kim screeches: 'Yer tosser! Yer reely think I'd called 'im *Stephen* after what that sod done to me. Yer know what he done to me yer twat.' She picks up *The Complete Book of Given Names* (first published as *A Family Treasury of Christian Names*) and hurls it at him, missing. The book lands beside a gas cylinder. 'Yer can bugger that for a game of soldiers, arserag.' She sobs a convulsive sob, takes up her coat from the sofa bed, rips its lining on a wingnut, totters on her two-inch platforms down the metal steps into the old quarry and turns to yell: 'I'm going out.'

Ralphy stands at the door of the caravan and watches her go. A helicopter chugs above them and all across the seaward horizon there move the blue macs of policemen. Kim stumbles parlously. The wind distends her coat and it flaps all round her, wildly. The wind pitches through her hair, sending the ends streaming out as if from beneath a tight cap. She is not wearing a tight cap; the hair on top of her head looks that way because it is dirty, fixed to her pointed skull with lard particles, grease from the sheets, sump filth from Ralphy's cracked, tenderly stroking hands. Ralphy has really

134

landed himself in it, hasn't he? You can't say he wasn't
warned. He was. But he liked the way she used to run her foot
up and down his calf when Steve was nodding off from too
much Guinness. He liked the way she owned to admiring his
looks, he liked the alliterative way she deprecated Steve's
conversation and implicitly lauded his: 'With 'im 's' all
fuckin' football 'n' fishin' frankly.' She sounded knowing,
worldly.

It wasn't love at first sight. First sight should have been a
warning; too bad for Ralphy that he didn't heed it. First sight
was of her holding a pan of blue-flaming beefburgers beneath
a tap; first sound was her screaming at her little boy Sean.
Then she shook Sean and told Steve to bugger off back down
the pub. The next time Steve took Ralphy back to the flat was
after the paraffin lorry had broken down and they had spent
three hours in the cab waiting for assistance. Steve had had
nothing to drink. Kim had; she was wearing the clogs of a
Carpaccian courtesan, a maroon ciré dress with a high slit,
fishnets, a garter that was round her ankle now. Her teeth
were the colour of her dress. Her lips were nearly beetroot.
She was dancing by herself to a powerful ballad of forbidden
love whined by a Nashville psycho. 'I been 'avin a party,
like,' she said to Steve who hit her in the mouth, thus adding
to the jumble of reds around it. 'Yer sod,' said Kim, 'I've just
been enjoyin myself.' 'Yeh, go shteady Shteve,' said Ralphy.

It had to happen. It happened one Saturday afternoon in
April. Steve was sent off in the twelfth minute for persistent
fouls on their number nine. No bath (water not hot yet), off-
licence (bottle of Bell's, six-pack of Special Brew), home.
Home early. The sequel is commonplace: Kim kneeling on
the kitchen floor, the bulge in her cheek, the cries, the
threats, the broken glass, the broken teeth, the broken home.
Ralphy ran down flight after flight of jarring stairs that stank
of urine and were sprayed with oaths and sexual boasts. Every
other flight culminated in thick wired glass, that's all there
was between Ralphy and a broken neck. That evening Steve
telephoned Ralphy and said he was going to kill him. Ralphy
took one of his mother's sleepers to help him get off. The next

day he told his mother it was a bad tummy, not his fear for his life, that had caused him to lose his appetite; he spent the day in his bedroom trying to make an Airfix model of a Flying Fortress. He was unable to concentrate; he got glue on his hands and they stuck to the greyish moiré curtain that he kept pulling back to survey the street. By tea time when Kim arrived the curtain was haphazardly ruched. Steve had turned Kim's face into a lump of bright colourful brawn that toned nice with the Elvis pink leatherette of the suitcase she clutched in front of her. Ralphy knows the contents of that case by heart now: the children's photos that are on the floor of the caravan behind him, an alopeciac teddy, a pair of fur-trimmed tangerine satin Sexciters, a half knitted cardigan, a seated skirt, a copy of Robert Redford's *The Great Gatsby*, two copies of *Family Circle*, a rabbit's foot keyring, what she thinks is called an isserpermander, lots of novel costume jewellery, laddered tights — nothing very special really, but all of it *hers* which lends it something. His mother wouldn't let her stay. They could hardly have stayed anyway; Steve telephoned more threats, his voice was hoarse, lifeless. He mocked Ralphy's appearance, told him he looked like a girl, told him his beard was bumfluff, told him: 'Wherever you shove it in 'er I been there first.' It sounded as though Steve had been crying; when he said 'I'm goina fuckin' castrate you,' Ralphy felt a medicine ball that had been hiding in his stomach force itself up into his throat.

They spent the first night at a guesthouse that was sur-rounded by market gardens. The bed was damp, the room smelled of decaying linoleum. Kim kept her face covered with a scarf, feigning maxillary sinusitis — Ralphy didn't want to be taken for a wife-beater, he didn't want any questions. In the shadow of cooling towers beside the swollen Trent, Ralphy part-exchanged the big Suzuki for a Ford Escort van; the cash adjustment bulged in the pocket of his motorcycle jacket on whose back were lettered in tarnished studs the names Saxon, Black Sabbath, Pagan Altar. Kim appreciated his sacrifice: 'That bike were 'is life.' She showed that she appreciated it by making him stop at a 'Bookshop' where she bought a black leather mask so that he would not have to look at her facial wounds at night. He loved her, he had a tattooist inscribe his right arm with the legend 'Kim. Till I Die.' The blueblack letters rose proud of his unmarked skin, he winced and bit his lip in an effort to conceal the pain. They drove south. Their hearts leapt when they were stopped on the edge of the Black Country at a police roadblock. But it was just that two zoo kangaroos had been found with their throats slashed. 'It'll put Dudley on the map,' said a constable looking (for what?) in the back of the van; he prodded Kim's suitcase, turned over the sleeping-bag: 'Where you going then?' As far from Steve as possible. Kim prayed that the policeman wouldn't look at her face. 'Evesham,' said Ralphy, reading from the back of a van. 'Ah,' said the policeman and waved them on. So Ralphy drove to Evesham. They stayed for a week. Ralphy worked for four days at a boatyard touching up the paint on children's paddle craft that had been scratched at Easter and had to be spruce for the Whitsun trade. Kim got up late, walked in the riverside gardens whose gateway is a whale's jawbone, shoplifted a pullover and a bottle of Cyprus sherry, and went to the cinema. They were happy. Ralphy telephoned his mother who told him that Steve and two of Steve's friends had come round twice. Did he know that *she* had two children and was ten years older than he was? Did he know that no good was going to come of it all? They drove south again. The roads were spangled with runover animals whose flesh and fur gaped at the world in pudendal conjunction. Hard shoulder crows loitered between meals. Every blue Cortina in the rearview mirror had Steve at its wheel. As he left a tobacconist's at Weston-Super-Mare Ralphy saw Steve watching him from a bus shelter. He told Kim that he felt like a secret agent.

Her face began to heal; she continued nevertheless to wear the mask. She stole something every day: a set of place-mats with castles on them, a torch, a lacquer cigarette-box, sunglasses, a typewriter ribbon, a leg of lamb (despite having no means of cooking it), a pair of Mexican dolls that she hung from the van's dashboard, a beach umbrella, an ironing-board cover, brightly coloured things mostly — she especially liked novelty matches. She never missed the children, never pined for them. Ralphy found work hard to come by. On Portland they rented a caravan.

Here's Douthey. Watch his hands work. They do what the immemorially refined trio of tongue and teeth and palate can do, but oh so slowly despite their frantic dance. (By the time you have reached the end of this paragraph all Douthey will have told Skip Laverack is that two people are in a car at the front of the hotel with a shotgun among their luggage.) Just watch his hands go: They're doing a formal display, an interpretative rumba; now they're cuddling rashly, pecking and petting; next thing you know they're the coupling limbs of illicit lovers. Look again: Douthey's right index trips across his southpaw's lines, it treads on love, chance, fortune, life.

Remember: (a) The conventional manual alphabet Douthey uses is rarely understood by anyone other than a fellow mute, Skip Laverack is an exception; (b) The pidgin mime Douthey and Skip Laverack use is peculiar to them. It is based on private jokes, old allusions. An hourglass traced in the air doesn't mean a woman, nor does it mean an hourglass; it means a large-scale fight like the one that, indeed, did begin over a busty tart at a New Year's Eve bash a dozen years ago; (c) Douthey's contact with the rest of the race is functional. Few people engage a mute in conversation even if he can lip-read. Douthey is used to that. He has his solaces no doubt. Ideas born of new words are not among them.

Two fingers in the mouth means a shotgun. Skip Laverack makes the gesture himself, just as one repeats a word that has possibly been misheard. A sign language is as liable as any other to go wrong, unparsed, provoke misunderstandings and malapropisms. Douthey nods affirmation, Skip Laverack shrugs and they walk towards the hotel. Douthey's big orbicular head with its fine baby-hair bobs about in the

138

blue dome. The sky here changes quickly, quicker than anywhere else; one moment it's 4B lead, the next it's all the shades of a monochrome photograph. Just now the bright blue is broken. Look, Douthey's looking – there, seriatim in the sky, are there fugitive cirrus clouds in the form and line of three flying ducks like those that people who live in houses are supposed to put on their walls. Douthey doesn't live in a house, he lives in a lean-to at the hotel. Douthey stares at them so intently it suggests he believes that they are the ducks on God's parlour wall, and that we are merely guests. Empyreal delusions like that are what you get if you have good eyesight and no one to talk to; gradually the ducks close up, conjoin in celestial sodomy and are turned, for their crime, into pyre and prisoner.

For as far as he can see there are dry-stone walls in a state of collapse; some are cairns now, others even less formed piles. The policemen in their dark blue macs climb awkwardly over them, their dogs trying to pull away across the coarse grass that is starred with more stones. Here and there great oolitic wedges rise from the ground like the stubs of megaliths; this ground is scarred, pitted, broken (there are craters everywhere). It could be the foundations of a city that was razed one night in a far age, a place on which a terrible revenge was exacted. And the houses that are scattered about this ruinous terrain are mean, grim, *urban*; terraces displaced from the soot towns and planted randomly. No trees grow here and the wind is unchecked, a bully; it strikes from anywhere, it must be blown by inconceivably bloated putti, it can make you mad, it gangs up with the wrong sort. The noise! – you turn and expect to see marquees billowing, sails slapping. Douthey can't hear it. He cannot even imagine what sound is like. He doesn't know that the gulls screech like men in their death throes, like children abandoned on a winter beach to die. And he doesn't know that Kim, who is just now passing on the other side of the wall pushing against the wind, is muttering. She is muttering awful things about Ralphy in particular and all men too. He does know that she is on the way to the lounge bar where she'll sit in front of the burning logs, concentrating on the flames and embers that have, in all likelihood, something to tell us all. He watches her with panda eyes. He can tell there's something wrong even though he didn't hear her cussing – he's got the gift. He needs it, for his ears are not really ears, just indecorative holes in the sides of his head; the external bits are there merely to dissemble his abnormality. His mouth is similar: It's an effective instrument for feeding and respiration, but not a sound comes from it. A sound *could* come from it. He was taught to speak once. The noises he made were weird, drainlike, pitiful – little belches for help. He tried so hard to please. His mothers and sisters laughed, shook their heads, his sisters brought their friends to listen. He stopped trying, he was shocked into what the nosology inaptly terms *elective* mutism. He has not spoken since. His mouth is also capable of kissing. Who wants to explore that silent cavity?

By contrast the mouths of the two people whose suitcases and shotgun he carries into the hotel work O.K. and emit foul words of expectation. It's just that these mouths *look* so wrong ...

The body of Chantal Keevil, who had been missing from home for three days, was spotted from the cliffs at Hallelujah Bay by a picnicking couple at noon on Thursday July 7. She lay at the bottom of an ineffably desolate funnel of waste stone hurled from the cliff top by convicts a hundred years before. She was naked and stewn with twisted wrack. Her legs were crossed to make a crude ampersand. Some of her hair had been cut. She had choked on shingle.

That evening Kevin Dickon telephoned his copy to his newspaper in London from the Ratings Mess at Castletown, where Chantal had lived with her parents in married quarters. When the copy was set it was found that there was a widow; this is printers' argot for a word that sits alone on a line at the end of a paragraph, such words are deemed unsightly. The sentence in question asked: 'Are the honest folk of this sturdy, historic isle to look on helplessly as their defenceless daughters are decimated by a brute?' 'Brute' was the offending word. A sub-editor (£11,250 plus yellow Toyota) thought hard about it, thought of all he knew of sex crimes, all he knew was what he had read in newspapers. He erased the question mark and added the qualification 'who stalks in a hood?' Kevin Dickon pushed toastcrumbs from his bad teeth with a matchstick and rued the size of his by-line. He had tipped Douthey £1 to go into Easton to buy the papers, had even sauntered out to meet the dummy as he pedalled uphill on the flat. And all he had to show for it was his name in eight-point – no flash saying 'Top Reporter', no photograph of his purposeful bandit moustache. He said to Skip Laverack: 'And one of those wretched noddies has put in that he wears a hood.' Skip Laverack swears that he put down the crossword he was doing, looked at the copy of Kevin's story on the bar and said that The Hooded Brute would be a good name. They had spent the greater part of the previous evening mulling over old times and toying with the nomenclatural formulae that such criminals demand. The best they had done was The Chesil Beast, but that sounded too much like a prize catch. Skip Laverack went back to his strenuously anagrammatic crossword; then he amended the adjective to 'hoody' – like the Hoody Crow that plucks out the eyes of baby lambs. Kevin Dickon straightaway telephoned Joyce Hand and begged an interview. It was published the next day, occupied an entire page, had photographs of Joyce Hand, of Susan's grave at St George, Reforne ('We Shall Not Forget You Darling'), and of Chantal Keevil. The headline was 'Grief Stricken Mother Says SAVE US FROM THIS HOODY BRUTE'. Kevin was billed as 'Star Newsman Kevin Dickon', and the screened headshot of him was as big as a fancy foreign stamp. He stayed for a further ten days. He paid Skip Laverack £20 per day instead of the usual £12.50 and got in return a daily receipt for £45. This is what friends are for. They played brag into the early hours. One day they sailed around the Bill from Balaclava Bay and back again. Kevin wrote two further stories, one about the inability of 150 policemen and 60 soldiers to find the murderer and another about the detrimental effects on tourism – 'Who'll Risk

Their Precious Ones On Death Coast?' The head at the top of these pieces was not Kevin's but that of a man wearing an executioner's hood.

The eve of his departure (to mine the human interest in the deaths in a bungalow fire at Biscarrosse Plage, Landes, of an English family), Kevin met Kim. She was at the bar and full of Emva and self-pity. She was pregnant: 'I'm bleedin' pregnant see. In *that* fuckin' doss. Pregnant. Sno 'ot water. Club, luv,' she said, 'for *seven weeks*. Cunt musta scored 'n 'ole in one just about. Can't get me cards for a termination see. 'Ave to pray frit.' But she couldn't afford to pay for it.

Anyway, she quite wanted it: 'Mind, if it's got Ralphy's eyes ... you only got to look at 'is eyes, 'e's got lovely eyes, Ralphy. Reel deep, Ralphy's eyes.' (Smoke – three Benson packs a day – got in *her* eyes.) And she dared not send for her N.H.S. cards lest Steve discover her whereabouts; this was a matter where she was inconsistent. She had had Ralphy take photographs of her with a Polaroid Colorpack 80 and send them to Readers' Wives in one of Steve's favourite magazines and D-I-Y-Hot-Shot in another, just to make Steve jealous. The set – the interior of a Firecrest Mark 3 Executive 2-Berth Open Plan – could not have made *anyone* jealous. They had posted the photographs at Ferndown on the way back from stock-car racing at Matcham's Park. She wouldn't have the figure for that sort of thing much longer. Kevin felt vague pity for her, bought her more drinks. She made conversation from gratitude: 'Bleedin' wind, never stops. It could make you funny.' He told her that the weather was worse in winter, that in winter there were fogs that used to avail wreckers, that in winter the people of this dismal isthmus who dared not say the word 'rabbit' used to keep warm by burning the excrement of their few cattle and their sheep. It gave Kim an idea.

Everything Kevin said about winter on Portland is right. It's no fun. Forget it, don't even bother to try it out, stay at home. Take my word for just how wretched it can be there. The sea is the colour of marine camouflage, of cigarette ash, of those gulls that make coathangers in the sky. The soil

142

drifts, like dust on a pavement, to reveal the rock beneath it. Stone triumphs all around you. Columnar whirlwinds of cement dust leap from the land. The rain stings like electricity. Thousands of millions of tons of pebbles on Chesil Bank groan in eternal attrition. We have here a landscape that is impervious to seasonal marks. There are no leaf piles, everything keeps grey and desolate. The wide stone streets on top of the rock are always shiny and sometimes the broken, quarried blocks gleam like relics in a giants' ossuary. No one visits the lighthouse, no one watches the rush of the murderous Race below. Kim and Ralphy noticed all this and more too. They stayed till the end, playing Name the Name, watching the baby stretch Kim, drinking and listening to the jukebox at Skip's. Ralphy did well with the logs, and with the bait at weekends.

St George, Reforne is swagger and dandiacal like a barefist beau. Under a tarmac sky Douthey killed a dog here, beating it with a stone, swinging it by the hind legs so it connected (occipital crunch, terminal howl) with the lichenous plinth of a dead sailor's urn. The dog's owners had abandoned it; it had gone wild, galloping blackly across fields, it had killed a sheep. Douthey adores sheep and the taste of their meat and the oiliness of their coats and their sweet compliant faces. He told Skip Laverack that a smallholder had paid him to get the dog; he carried it from the graveyard and left it on a crude roadside gatepier. 'I shaw Douthey', said Ralphy to Skip Laverack, 'givin' a dog whatfor yeshterday.' 'It was a danger to children,' replied Skip Laverack, and Ralphy blushed. 'Shpose so,' he said. Kim and Clark (that week if he was a boy he was Clark) swayed in time to 'Stand By Your Man'. Kim shut her eyes for the line 'And show the world you love him.' She was moved by songs of honour and duty. Ralphy bought drinks all round. Little Clark's rudimentary limbs wriggled. 'Oohwh, there 'e goes again. 'E's a real little groper, jus' like 'is dad.' And Ralphy blushed again, and put his hand on Kim's shoulder in one of the many uxurious gestures he made every day now; he was a proud paternal man now.

Follow him as he provides for Kim and Candy (a week has passed). His van moves slowly, effortfully, uphill through Fortuneswell, past the place where Susan Hand lived and died, into bottom gear, its body low over the wheels, its back full to the roof with trunks and boughs; the noise is a monotone screech till he reaches the plain. Later there is another monotone screech, that of the old paraffin-motor saw with which he turns the wood into cylinders. There are logs piled all round the caravan, logs beneath it ('Stopped some of the rising draughts, like. Made it warmer,' – Kim, careless), logs covered in tarpaulin to look like bothies. There is not the demand for logs that Kim promised; her assumption that people here still warmed their dour houses with dung was wrong. Ralphy has cut his prices. Competitive, certainly, but unprofitable too. Ralphy relies ever less on offcuts from timber merchants; increasingly he seeks ordered windfall, i.e. the neat piles of coniferous trunks that are found on Forestry Commission land, piles whose nocturnal depletion goes unseen Ralphy learns to keep late hours. At night he goes to Wareham Forest, to the woods near Clyffe House (where he gets Dutch Courage in a Hollywood-English pub), to Ilsington Wood (where in spring there are cliffs of rhododendron high as houses – Ralphy is going to miss that sight); he goes about his business quietly, thoroughly. Sometimes it is past 5 a.m. before he is home, and then he sleeps foetally curled on the floor by the door rather than disturb Kim, who'll whine and moan then, and *really create* in the morning. Ralphy is stealing for three. He drives the van along tyrefelt paths where rabbits pop up in the lights. He directs a torch from the open windows; he breathes white breath into the wood and it clouds the light beam. Now and again and again that beam strikes a pile. He lifts it with such foraging zeal that he can never hear the perpetual rustling of small stealthless animals. When he has finished and he puts his hands to the steering-wheel they wet it with blood, and stick to it. The mist effects in this scene have been extravagant. Picture the mist lassooing a tree, and making the crisp pig of moon into a soft-focus blob, and turning into the spilled stuffing of a million mattresses in front of the van's lights. Ralphy drives at walking speed, his damaged hands alert for signs that the track is boggy. He still gets stuck. There is impotent mechanical roaring, and mud flecks everything. Once when he got stuck he put logs beneath the tyres, a tip learnt from television, a wrong tip actually – that night he had to abandon most of his load; that was frustrating. What happened at Decoy Heath in the middle of December was worse than frustrating. Ralphy peers ahead of him. There is a Transit van parked across the track, its doors open towards the blue wood, its headlights shining into a plantation of young trees. Ralphy thinks there has been an accident and gets out of his van. He need not have bothered to get out, they'd have pulled him out. One of them clubs him with a spade, another swings a Christmas Tree whose roots graze his face, the earth from whose roots fills his eyes. He is kicked as he lies in the mud. No one speaks a word. There are merely grunts. He hardly sees his assailants, can recall only a shape 'like a chimney' and the gusts of white all about it. There are two of them, maybe four. In the morning Kim finds him asleep on the floor. His upper lip is swollen like a pasty. The thumb-length gash on his cheek is filthy, cross-hatched with pine needles; it requires a row of high relief stitches. His face is as blotchy and colourful as a plucked pheasant. His trousers are damp to the knees with the excrement of a moment's fright.

Ralphy walks the terrible grey rampart of the Chesil Bank; his wounded face is smothered against the killer wind and he clutches two buckets in each hand. The buckets contain fish heads and fish entrails, got from the oily quay near the Custom House and from fishmongers and supermarkets; lumps of squid, mackerel, herring (same sources); tins of luncheon meat and pet food (Cash & Carry, using Skip Laverack's discount ticket); lugworms (dug at dawn near the Western Ledges). He peddles this stuff to the fishermen who crouch, quilted against the wintry spray, sixty feet below him and – but this must be a perspectival joke – below the level of the insistent sea. The Chesil Bank rises from the sea like

the infinite roof of a submerged primitive palace. God does
not know how many stones comprise it. It may be the work of
generations of a forgotten race of diligent, literal minded
dyke-people who believed that the sea might be kept at bay if
they threw stones at it. Along the beach this afternoon are
717 fishermen (information from the brewery sponsoring the
Christmas Championship and giving prizes of £740 – confirmed by *Angler's Mail*). That is a lot of fishermen. It is just
Ralphy's luck that Steve should be among them, just
Ralphy's luck that Steve should be the one to cause a crowd to
gather round him, that Steve should hook a seagull. Ralphy
is a dozen pegs away selling Go-Cat and mackerel to a
despondent baldy when it happens. Of course he has no idea
it is Steve. He hurries along the beach behind two match
officials, past carbon rods, tackle boxes, vacuum flasks,
umbrellas (useless here), spare reels, spools of line, keep-
nets, landing-nets, folding stools, whole cut-loaves made
into sandwiches, weights, beer cans, etc. He hurries back.
(He has pushed through the anoraks surrounding the man
who remotely controls the gull flapping in the baby breakers,
flapping like the father of that first fish which made the move
into the air; this gull will never fly again. Ralphy is about to
proffer worthless matey advice when the struggling fisherman looks up at him). He really does hurry back, all sorts of
things are happening in his stomach and windpipe. He
scrambles up the Bank, bruising himself wantonly. When he
reaches the top and turns he can see that Steve is still playing
the gull. Steve has all the time in the world. Poor gull. Poor
Ralphy.

Poor Ralphy empties his buckets as he crunches back to his
van. Every time he looks behind him he sees scarey figures
whose progress is unaffected by the pebbles, every time he
looks behind him he stumbles to his knees. In his haste he
reverses his van into a low wall; he does not get out of the car
to examine the damage. He drives into Fortuneswell and
turns into backstreets where he will be safe from Steve's
pursuing car – he is prone to such quarry habits. He drives
carelessly, goes too close to a cyclist tacking up the terraced

146

hill towards the prison. Ralphy finds that the road is blocked by two fire engines. Smoke the colour of earwax is rolling out of an upstairs window. Spectators crowd the pavements. A fireman with a face specially fattened to give children bad dreams put that face to his and told him to turn back. The sirens of police cars and ambulances must have disturbed nearly everyone in that part of the town. The police will be back later, on other business.

Now, Jocky Hogg's mouth. 'I gotta mouth like a nun's minge.' That's what he says, that's how his mouth *feels*, it's not how it looks. It looks to you and me and Skip Laverack and Douthey like a wound, a crass incision in a face that, genetically deficient, needed a slit put in it. It looks to Skip's bimbo Lucy Guest like a complicated knitting stitch. (Girls' talk.) I believe it *is* inherited; Jocky's daughter Dale has it too, that wound, that bad mouth. I believe the worst of anyone with a mouth like that. They are not mouths that you want to watch: Jocky tips whisky into his and some of it comes straight out and down his jowl and on to his maroon pullover with the bobbly lime-green legend, JOCKY HOGG. Dale slams her glass against his, 'Chiss, Dad – good 'untin'. 'Ere's to the jackpot.' 'Tha's spirit,' says Jocky and wanders into reception to watch Douthey bring in their suitcases and the shotgun from the car. Who are these people? What do they want? What are they doing here?

It was the murder of Deborah Swift that Sunday, a week before Christmas, that brought Kevin Dickon back to Portland. Her head had been held in a coal scuttle in her grandmother's living room and the dust had asphyxiated her. Dickon offered Detective Superintendent Fowler who was leading the investigation a drink (two bottles of Hine) and hinted that he would write favourably about him – interested in people and society, reads poetry (Housman for the hangings, I'll bet). He got in return the exclusive quote: 'This maniac has nerves of high tempered steel. While he carried out this bestial act, this inhuman act, the street beneath was ringing with the bells of fire engines and the sirens of police cars. He perpetrated this act as though oblivious.'

Fowler said exactly the same to all the other reporters who offered him a drink; that set Kevin against him. He wrote a story about police incompetence. And when, the day after Boxing Day, Lesley Scofield, who was nine years old, was found dead, mutilated and partially scalped on the former railway track near Folly Pier, Kevin's paper had a field day – and so, later, did several M.P.s, every national newspaper save the other ones owned by the same group, the Press Council, countless bishops, social workers, actors and so on. The front page on December 28 (which falls in a conventionally poor week for news) read thus:

£20,000 £20,000 £20,000 £20,000 £20,000
RID US OF THE HOODY BRUTE
The Paper That Puts Its Money Where Its Heart Is
PORTLAND MANIAC CLAIMS FOURTH VICTIM
The Concerned Paper Pledges £20,000
GET HIM !!!!!!!!!

You see what Jocky Hogg is up to. This is a man that wants value from a newspaper. Go into the office of AAA Haulage (Kettering) Ltd in the morning and you'll find Jocky reading (say) the *Sun*. Go back just before he closes at 5.30 and he is still reading it, the same copy, he takes that long to read it. (Go there now and you won't find Jocky – he isn't out yet.) He reads it all: weather in Durban, small print in advertisements, cartoons, programmes on Welsh T.V., recipes, letters. He gazes at the word puzzle – 'Yesterday's solution: Frying Tonight.' He reads his stars half a dozen times – 'Accept all invitations, don't get stuck in a rut. A surprise activity could have interesting results. You may be receiving money from an unusual source.' He believes everything that he reads. He is the ideal reader. You'll see that he really believed he was going to 'win' £20,000. He is convinced he won it. This is a letter he wrote me in which he confirms that. 'You don't get that many chances coming your way, especially when you get to my age – be kind and just say I'm on the

148

wrong side of 50! You just want to grab the ones that do. Grab them and hold them. I don't mind telling you I had nightmares for months. Ironically they had to put me in along with a fellow that was hard of hearing because I woke up screaming all the time! No way wouldn't I do the same again. By and large I've got a clean conscience as God's my witness. There is no question in my mind, repeat NO QUESTION that I was RIGHT. Time has shown that I was, over and over, no question about that. Natural justice had its way – as you probably know I got literally thousands of letters. All backing me to the hilt, and I still get quite some, regularly. That blood group stuff was all got up. No one checked the tests. It was just their word that it didn't match. If there had been an independent test it would have been different.' His handwriting is small, neat, fluent. The paper is unlined.

Half an hour after their arrival at the hotel, during which time Douthey had served them a couple of drinks and they had wished good afternoon to Kim who was watching children's programmes on television, Jocky and Dale put the shotgun beneath a raincoat on the backseat of the car and drove out into the murk, looking. At the Bill a man whom Jocky attempted to question turned away towards the rocky ledges. A shopkeeper at Southwell said: 'Is there anything else? I'm closing now.' They drove slowly past rows of uncurtained, just lighted front-rooms where children played among broken streamers and torn tinsel decorations. Dale says that her father felt he had been sent to protect all Portland children. 'Bugger off, there's a good love,' said a petulant T.V. man on top of a Land Rover who was trying to get four policemen to walk across a field without tripping on the stones, 'we've got to get this before the light goes.' A fifth policeman, who was not included in the shot because his lack of moustache would have unbalanced it, told Jocky: 'Waste of time idn't it. With ones like this you find he'll get caught on the job or his missus'll have her suspicions ... I tell you what – 's'no bleedin' use having us marchin' all over the shop. 'S'all for the media like, the press boys and this lot.'

Later, with the last of the light, there was drizzle. The car slewed and skidded when Jocky braked to avoid a tractor and its unlit trailer parked between St George, Reforne and the hotel; Jocky walked down the road to address the driver. The tractor's rudimentary cab was empty. Jocky stamped like a little boy and shrugged towards Dale. He walked on to the tufty verge, looked over the dry stone wall. Ralphy, heaving logs in the old quarry, saw the figure appear above the ragged wall like a mountain giant and scampered into the caravan and pulled back the plastic curtain of the kitchenette to peer through the window at its daunting silhouette. Flame comes from the giant's hand, lights up his ogrish mouth. It is too far away for Ralphy to be able to discern any features, and, anyway, water droplets from his panic-stricken insides congregate on the pane to occlude his sight; he holds the plastic fuselage of a model Lancaster that hangs by nylon thread from the ceiling and aims it at the mountains. Jocky put his lighter back in his car coat pocket and waited a bit to see what else was going to happen down there. Then with his hair dewy and his hands aching he shuffled back to the car and Dale's warnings about head colds.

Jocky introduced himself to Kevin early that evening. He took from his wallet some scraps of brittle saffron newspaper that sprang into ruffs when unfolded. 'I was,' said Jocky, 'a real name to reckon with in the heyday of British ice hockey.' Kevin looked at him in wonder. 'Tha's how I found where you was staying, Kevin.' He held out for Kevin's inspection a ruff headlined 'Hogg The Matchwinner Again'. (Here is the source of Jocky's belief in newspapers.) 'You see who that's by, look — the name there.' 'Douglas Munro ... ah Duggie Munro, I know Duggie.' 'Tha's it, Kevin. Duggie 'n' me, we were like tha'. He had a real feel for the game. Great writer, still is. We keep in touch you know. So I rung him up, asked him to find out where you're staying. And here I am, in the flesh. We're goin' to work together on this one Kevin, tha's spirit.' Kevin Dickon gaped incredulously at the man whose hand gripped his shoulder, whose wrong mouth breathed warm dyspepsia over him. 'We're going to do it ain't we Dad,' said Dale, leaning across the lounge table, 'we're really gointa make it hot for him. You watch if we don't Kevin. Chiss.'

The photograph shows (l. to r.) Douthey, Dale, Jocky, Lucy Guest, Skip Laverack. Douthey wears a dark blazer and a white shirt buttoned to the collar, no tie. The others look outdoorsy – jerkins, oilproofs, straps and zips. Dale's hair blows across her face, sparing the three million readers the sight of her mouth. Behind them is part of the hotel, a harsh ashlar place whose sash windows are almost flush to its walls. Above them is the headline: 'THE FEARLESS FIVE: Big Hearted Readers Take Up Our £20,000 Challenge'. The photograph was published on Friday December 30, it was taken the previous afternoon and only Jocky failed to stare into the lens. He stared beyond it, beyond Burwood the fractious photographer, beyond Kevin who hugged himself against the cold. He stared at Ralphy hurrying away against the wind towards the horizon made by the dazzling white sea, Ralphy with his spindly legs and leather jacket and his arm round Kim, Ralphy with his cracked hands and the hardly healed gash on his face – who cut him?

'Who cut you Jimmy?'

'Eh? ... Oh ... a fellow. *No* – I don't wanna be in it. Don't like being in photos.' Ralphy said that to Kevin Dickon. 'And Kim don't neither, all right?'

'Are you sure?'

'I do. I'm gonna be in it,' said Kim, watching her face come to life with paint in the mirror above the lounge-bar fire. ''Mallright in photos, don't look dumpy like.'

'Why did this fella cut you? He must hae cut you for something.'

'The more heads we have in it the better so far as I'm concerned but it's up to you.'

'You fuckin' not gonna be in it Kim.' He spoke to her again, in a whisper. He was sure he knew how Steve had traced them.

151

'I said,' said Jocky, 'this fella got to have a reason; if it was a fella ... '

'Whash it got to do with you?'

'Yah windy twat. Are. Aren't you? I look nice in photos. You know I do Ralphy.'

'She wants to be in the photo,' Jocky blew whisky and shag reek at Ralphy. 'Ladies love to have their photos taken. ''Sfuckin' genius of the camera – turns a lady into a *goddess.*'

'Kim don't want to be in it.'

'You oughta be in it too an' all. You got nothing to hide have you. Pretty boy like you with your little cut there. 'T 'll be a dinky little scar.' Jocky made to stroke the weal with his cigarette hand and Ralphy looked at him as he had once at Steve – his eyes promised mallets and knives.

Jocky said: 'Everyone likes to have their pictures in the paper. 'Snatural. And we're kinda heroes. Y'know tha'. Hunters – the ones who got The Hoody Brute. The ones tha' – ai – the ones tha' claimed the scalp o' The Hoody Brute, whoever he is.'

Douthey tapped on the window and signalled that the photographer was ready; his excited mime was that of a wicked child playing at Peeping Tom. Ralphy took Kim by the arm and led her outside, away across the garden and the fields. Jocky followed him, as I said, with his eyes; he was going to follow Ralphy for ever. He asked Skip Laverack questions about Ralphy: When did he come to Portland? Why did he not want his photograph in the paper? Who is he? What does he do for a living? Why does he hide in the caravan when he realises that he is being observed? And so on. He had Skip Laverack ask Douthey the same questions. He himself asked them of Lucy Guest. He and Dale pored over cuttings of the case. He drove to the house of Bowns the allotment holder who had seen the lights of a car in the lane behind the building society office; Bowns agreed that it might have been a van. He drove to the police station at Fortuneswell and demanded an interview with Detective Superintendent Fowler. The desk sergeant spoke wearily into an internal telephone and told Jocky to wait. Just over an hour later a constable replaced the sergeant at the desk and when Jocky asked him he replied that Fowler had left twenty minutes before. Jocky kicked the wainscot, stamped upon the stone chip floor: 'Wha sorta' geg's he tryin' ta pull. He knew, he knew I had information ta gie him. *I'm on to something.*' Later Jocky and Dale drove across the dark plain to the rather grander hotel (Michelin, Pevsner) where Kevin Dickon had gone to drink with a group of reporters who were staying there. Dale had put on her best straight skirt with a cerise and emerald satin blazer and her sunburst motif platform boots. Kevin introduced Jocky as 'the one who played for Motherwell' and referred to the men with him as 'my colleagues'; they all had problems with their hair or their ages. They talked resentfully, enviously, of men that Jocky and Dale had never heard of. Jocky bought them lots of drinks. He followed Kevin to the lavatory, told him of his suspicions. Kevin grunted dismissively and slapped the towel machine. Before he went to bed Jocky walked to the caravan. There was no light in it and the Ford Escort van was not there. He crouched beside a pile of stones watching. The next night the scene was different.

Jocky and Dale spent a long time over breakfast, staining the surrounds of their kindred mouths with yolk, jam, fat. Dale rued the way that her hair obscured her face in the photograph; Jocky was pleased with his likeness and kept turning to it. Douthey pulled a sack of logs into the dining room, pointed to the newspaper and posed like a crucified man. As Jocky was going out at lunchtime Skip Laverack explained to him that Douthey was actually aping the figure of Justice; Jocky accepted this as a compliment. At the fire station none of the officers to whom he talked in the canteen could recall what vehicles they had seen in the area of the fire they had attended twelve days previously. Why not try Our Jacko? Our Jacko is the one who'd know if anyone did. Jocky found him in a dingy, ill-frequented public house near the gates of the Borstal. Our Jacko was by the fireplace — a failed Odeon of swirling butterscotch tiles. His body porked through the folds of a Windsor chair, auxiliary cheeks lay on his collar. He remembered a van whose driver, when instructed to turn round, had 'made a real three-course meal of it'. He agreed to meet Jocky at the hotel that night.

They walked together along the unlit road. The sea rumbled like a far-off train and there was not a star to be seen. Our Jacko cursed chronically, found breath hard to come by, wheezed, stubbed his toe and cried to God; he peers down into the quarry, there is a light in the caravan, and a slow shadow. The Ford van is there (it has been there since Ralphy arrived home from delivering logs late last night) but Our Jacko cannot see it clearly enough to say whether it is like the one he saw in the road where the fire was; awkwardly he climbs the wall with Jocky alongside him. A car driving towards the mainland illumines them, dazzles Our Jacko, who is proceeding back first, causing him to slip and yell again, causing Ralphy to peer out at twin giants, one bigger than the other. By the time that Kim reaches the window there is no one to be seen. Our Jacko and Jocky note the light switched off in the caravan and continue round the edge of the quarry. Ralphy catches sight of their bulks intermittently, Kim whines that she wants the light back on because she has got to a really exciting bit. After the figures disappear on the far side of his van Ralphy does not see them again, but it is another twenty minutes before he allows Kim to put on the light.

'Couldn't be more certain,' says Our Jacko, 'I thought to myself he'll be lucky if he gets away with no stop-light and his tail-light all cracked like that. Skol mate, that's very generous of you — mustn't go too much on the piss tonight mind, spoil it for tomorrow. I tell you, anyone calls us out then, they'll be lucky. I don't mind telling you, fire like the one where I seen chummy's van couldn't have come at a better time, makes people most forthcoming with the seasonal beverages. Must be a bit of an Ernie, don't you think, driving round with a motor in that condition.' You can say that again, Our Jacko.

Whoops! On New Year's Eve at about ten o'clock —

timecheck: five tartan knifeboys have just begun playing maudlin guitars on the full volume telly in the lounge bar. At just *after* ten, then, Kim's legs move without her asking them to and she and little Barrington inside lean away from Ralphy with whom they've been dancing a gauche slow. They lean too far backwards for Ralphy's arms to help, so far backwards that they sit on the Christmas tree that Douthey got and make the uprooted thing lie on its side in its tub.

She and Ralphy have been drinking with Lucy Guest since early afternoon. Ralphy was so jeffed then that he was asleep on the floor when Douthey brought them in some cake and some of the little sausages he was roasting for the evening; Kim let Douthey lie on the sofa beside her and put his head to her tummy. The thumps of two hearts, the foetal one cantering ahead, transmitted themselves to his temple. The discordant rhythms drowsed him and she had to tap his pink and yellow crown when the weight became too much for her. Lucy Guest complained that the cake was dry, and Kim poured white rum over it, lit it and laughed as Douthey's exhalations failed to put out the flames: "E 'uffed and 'e puffed and *still* they kept flickerin' ... ' She stroked his hair and he turned his head to her with such spaniel devotion. He made his hands dance a moment, then shrugged at her incomprehension and smiled.

Kim is now supine on the Christmas tree and shreds of glass coloured like old sweet wines and precious metals surround her. She looks surprised. The thirty or so people in the room have been there long enough to react, initially, as a *party*. Thus there is an indefinite time in which no one utters a word, the tartan louts tell you how sad life can be, and the true squalor of all collective sensation is fixed in an open-mouthed tableau. One, two — let's go again. Ralphy stumblingly tries to pick her up. He moves with exaggerated daintiness, as if on a highwire. He falls off. Down and down he goes, and when his right hand lands it is on the toothy conic top of a frosted-glass torch. It wasn't till Skip Laverack and one of Dale's sailors had lifted Kim to her feet that anyone saw how profusely his thumb ball bled. He was so drunk that the message didn't reach his brain – he hadn't shrieked, he thought that he had made contact with a crown cork on the floor, that was all. Now there was blood (AB, commonplace, red) down his pale trousers and Lucy Guest and Dale round him and leading him to the kitchen and the joint-stiffening cold tap and the burning, limpet ice-cubes. They wrapped his hand in gauze and a tea-towel. Lucy Guest gave him a smacker on his mouth and told him he ought to take Kim home. He nodded and a cataract of aloes brown vomit (drinking on an empty stomach, son) jumped out of his just kissed mouth. Lucy Guest wiped him clean with a J-Cloth. When he went back into the bar the roar was like a high oven's. He caught Jocky's eye and smiled doltishly. Dale agreed to walk them back to the caravan, she was glad to get away from the groping sailors for a while. Skip Laverack kissed Kim and he kissed Ralphy and made them wait outside in the foggy cold (they were anaesthetised against that too) while he fetched them a bottle of Teacher's 'to see the new one in with'. He kissed them both again.

Ralphy held his hand across his chest, stiffly, in the position that small girls put the bandaged limbs of their dolls; Dale refused to go by way of the fields. She kept her arm round Kim, and Ralphy sang, and gambolled with the whisky bottle at his mouth, doing a strutting idol's jig. He fell twice and the macadam belted him. What a picture they made! Dale almost carrying Kim and the baby, Ralphy getting the words wrong, reeling. What a picture, a bad impressionist picture, a sensitive Sunday daub of skittles wrapped in steam and antimony. Ralphy crowed in the fog: 'I'm the cock of the yard, I'm the cock of the yard, I'll give yer a yard of cock, I'll give yer a yard of cock.' Dale told him: 'You're disgusting.' He war-danced round her and pressed his good hand against her bottom.

The caravan smelled of frying. Dale helped Ralphy pull out the sofa bed in whose central fold was a sheet so creased and knotted it looked like one used to escape down the wall of a building. Kim lay down without taking off her clothes or shoes and Ralphy put the eiderdown over her and sat down beside her, clutching his whisky between his forearm and his trunk, pulling at Dale's coat. She pushed him away: 'I could do with some of that.' She was looking at an open tin of instant coffee. There were little piles of the coffee powder, hardened with condensation like rodent droppings, on every horizontal surface. But despite what was said the caravan wasn't all that dirty. ''elpshelf,' said Ralphy. Dale turned her back to him and lit the gas. Fragments of the alkaline crust in the mucky kettle rattled; she filled it from a water can that was almost empty. Ralphy caught her this time; she toppled on to the bed beside him and he put his hand beneath her skirt. She was free with a brusque wriggle: 'Bleedin' octopus aren't you. I can do without it. Thanks ever so.' Ralph drank as if from a porron. Kim emitted a vibrato snore and he turned to cuddle her. Dale's hair became entangled with a Spitfire that hung from the ceiling. She tipped the boiling water into a cup whose handle was reduced to two matt lugs, it was too hot to hold. She sniffed a couple of milk bottles. 'Got any that's not off?' she asked. But Ralphy was asleep; his mouth was limp and his bandaged hand was on Kim's hair. She opened a cupboard to see if there was a fresh bottle of milk in it (so she says). It was full of bright knick-knackery that Kim had stolen, silly useless trifles – tin birds, a plate with the Queen's face on it, plastic clothes for a doll, a verisimilar Friesian cow-creamer. She shut it just in time to stop the stuff falling to the floor and opened another, this one at head height above the Butane gas heater. Crumpled clothes unwound and sprung over her shoulders. Ralphy stirred and grunted. She stooped to gather the garments, giggled when she saw what they were. They were the clothes from the Lovewear International mail catalogue that Kim had worn in the Polaroid photographs: a satin Basque, a tasselled G-string, a mauve nightie trimmed with fake fur, a black suspender belt trimmed with carmine satin, a pair of open-crotch briefs which also had holes for two legs and one catheter, several pairs of stockings, a garter, black gloves that might reach the upper arm, studded leather bracelets and collar. (They had not all been worn in the same photograph.)

There was also a white shirt into which Dale bundled the other things; she stood on a flimsy folding chair and pushed the lot into the cupboard. It was then that she saw at the back of the cupboard the black leather mask that Kim had bought all those months ago. Dale looked down at the sleeping brute, gingerly put the mask in her pocket, extinguished the lamp, locked the caravan door, hurled the key across the quarry, and ran back to the hotel as well as she could. A wind had blown up now, and the fog had gone. The night now is black as a coma.

I guess you know the rest. You know how Jocky, Dale and the drunken sailor (who was a friend of Chantal Keevil's father) drove to the caravan. You know how Douthey saw them go – Dale at the wheel, Jocky with the twelve-bore beside her, the drunken sailor with his head out of the window over Jocky's shoulder. You know how Douthey signalled his fears to Skip Laverack. Douthey, at the far end of the room from Skip Laverack, traces an hourglass in the smokey air. (Chorus of revellers: 'Feeling the need is he?') He puts two fingers in his mouth. (Chorus of revellers: 'Wanting a bit of La Frog is he? Ooo la la!') In the middle of the room their hands sprint with a precision rare in that mass of spinning limbs. Why did they take so long? The site of the caravan is little over half a mile from the hotel, a minute's drive – it was just Ralphy's luck that Skip Laverack's car should be surrounded by those of his customers. The two men hurried across the fields, tripping persistently, turning their ankles, prey to all the stony pratfalls earth and night could muster. By the time they got to the quarry the flames were finding their own feet, sensibly learning to walk before they skipped, before they ran hither and thither among the logs, multiplying themselves in lithe gestures of spontaneous generation – Jocky was, say, merely their godfather or a proud obstetrician.

Mark, this was not what Jocky had intended. He wanted to confront Ralphy with the leather mask, and Dale free-

158

wheeled the last hundred yards down the track to the quarry. She need not have bothered for it would take much more than engine noise to wake them. They made their way through log piles and beat roughly on the door, Jocky aiming the gun at it with the mask over the muzzle; there was no answer, not a sound inside. The drunken sailor walked around the caravan, striking its panels with a treetrunk. Dale's fists were clenched, she shook with excitement. Ralphy, who had little left to discover save that flames sting rather than lick, probably dreamed of a great storm.

It is hard to say who started it: the sailor's feet unwittingly kicked the jerrycan of paraffin that stood by the motor-saw; Dale had a lighter; Jocky was increasingly frustrated that his yells and taunts brought no answer. It was surely Jocky that doused the logs that Ralphy had stacked beneath the caravan: he was holding the empty can in one hand and the gun in the other when Douthey and Skip Laverack arrived. Before you could say 'good servant, bad master', the flames grew up into strapping adult hooligans. It was all very lively: the spluttering irate yaps turned into a roar; the resinous smell was sat on by one that was determined to scrape your nostrils. The wind was in league with our three happy arsonists, it made them into murderers with just a few judicous puffs. Black things like ill-made bats flapped up to the sky and great grey bushes swayed to reveal jitterbugging ghosts in citrus shrouds. The paint crazed and bubbled and Kim's head came to a window. This is when Douthey goes in. He forces the door with a stake, thus making an aperture that allows the wicked wind to do its stuff and lets out a horrible cry of Ralphy's, whose dreamtime pandemonium is, on waking, the real thing. The flames are topless now, like those of wreckers' fires; they can be seen at the hotel where Lucy Guest rings the fire brigade – Our Jacko was right, they were all drunk. Even after Douthey brings out Kim, Dale goes on jumping in delirious spasms. As Douthey gets free of Skip Laverack and goes through the bright wall for Ralphy the roof sighs and falls like a drunk – slow-motion, sagging. A side panel pops out and there, that's Ralphy. The last thing Ralphy saw was Jocky

Hogg's damp mouth. That is one of the awful things about being murdered, the last thing you see is someone who hated you that much.

There were no more little girls killed.

Kim's son was born premature at 11.07 a.m. on January 1, 197– at Portwey Hospital. It's a boy, Ralphy. She remained on Portland till he was almost a year old, living in an attic at Skip Laverack's hotel. The last I heard of her she had gone back to Evesham, I think she was working as a waitress. She must have wheeled her baby through the whale's jawbone into the dark gardens where she was so happy beside Ralphy. She is supposed to have moved again since then – the Welsh Marches, somewhere there. The boy must be at school now. She gave him the names Ralph and Rob, the latter after Douthey who saved them and who lost his hands when the blazing roof fell on them as he tried to rescue Ralphy; he can't talk at all now – what would he tell us if he could, poor Douthey? That's his name, Rob, Rob Douthey. What do you make of that name? What's in it? What's in such a name?

Tonight I'll win at Scrabble. Watch me now.

Lightning Source UK Ltd.
Milton Keynes UK
UKHW041530260221
379394UK00001B/127